UNMASKED

A DE-EXTINCT ZOO MYSTERY

CAROL POTENZA

Tiny
MAMMOTH

PRESS

ISBN: 978-1-7363262-2-0 (ebook); 979-8-9867690-1-1 (paperback)

PUBLISHED BY TINY MAMMOTH PRESS

website: www.carolpotenza.com

EDITOR: COLLEEN WAGNER

PROOFREADER: GILLY WRIGHT

COVER: BRANDI DOANE MCCANN

THE DE-EXTINCT ZOO MYSTERY SERIES

Veterinarian Milly Smith works in a zoo surrounded by resurrected Ice Age megafauna—mammoths, woolly rhinos, giant short-faced bears, enormous apes—brought to life by de-extinction geneticists. They may be fine playing god, but Milly cares deeply for each and every creature living in the Pleistocene BioPark.

When a series of murders threaten her flock, Milly is drawn into the investigations. Except the murders are only pieces in a deadly game. One Milly doesn't even know she's playing.

UNMASKED

Catch the Killer, Save the Bear

Veterinarian Milly Smith is living her dream, working in a zoo populated by de-extinct creatures resurrected from ancient DNA: Mammoths and mastodons, dire wolves and do-dos, camelops and sabre-toothed cats.

But a routine surgery on a massive short-face bear goes horribly wrong and a colleague is dead. The bear is slated to be destroyed unless Milly can prove the animal was used by a diabolical killer as a murder weapon.

A killer whose attention has turned to Milly.

DEDICATION

For Leos, Marcus, and Laura, who gamely climbed in the truck when I wanted to visit Kilbourne Hole, Prehistoric Trackways, Three Rivers Petroglyphs, and crumbling Louisiana graveyards on the hottest days of July.

THE PLEISTOCENE EPOCH'S ASSASSIN

Pleistocene BioPark, a Zoological Wonder of the World
De-extinct Bear Grotto

[*Printed on the display above the* Arctodus simus *exhibit*]

The short-faced bear (*Arctodus simus, Tremarctinae ssp*) is now the largest bear in the world! The original *A. simus* bears at the Pleistocene Zoological Park were genetically engineered on a DNA platform from the South American spectacled bear (*Tremarctos ornatus*), its closest living relative. It even shares the same markings—a white face mask or spectacles around the eyes.

With adult males weighing in at over a ton (~1,000 kilograms) and standing as much as 12 feet (3.6 meters) on hind legs, short-faced bears can stare a 6-foot-tall (1.8 meters) human in the eye when on all fours. Not only do they differ substantially in size from modern-day bears, their long limbs and forward-facing feet allow them to run at speeds of up to 30 mph (50 kph), faster than most horses.

Short-faced bears first appeared in the fossil record around 1.6 million years ago and were driven to extinction approximately 11,000 years ago at the end of the last Ice Age, probably due to excessive hunting and competition by human immigrants crossing the Beringia land bridge into North America over 13,500 years ago.

Once North America's top predator, short-faced bears were solitary, with an olfactory organ that could smell a rotting carcass up to 6 miles (10 km) away. Their enhanced sense of smell allowed them to practice kleptoparasitism—bullying other animals into giving up their prey. These bears would eat almost anything, making them omnivorous like modern brown and grizzly bears.

But a bear this size must ultimately kill to survive, and they preyed on hoofed mammals present in astonishing abundance on the grassy plains of Pleistocene North America. Because of their large size, they needed to consume up to 40 lbs. (18 kg) of meat a day. If a human did see one, they were already too close to this Pleistocene assassin, whose claws slashed flesh to disembowel and jaws crushed bone to powder.

CHAPTER ONE

SENIOR VETERINARY resident Milly Smith rested her upper body against the huge, sedated prehistoric bear's side. She sank into the thick woolly fur, arms spread like embracing wings, ear pressed to the bear's chest, absorbing the strong thumps of its heart. Milly closed her eyes and combed ungloved fingers down Maskwa's flank, the pungent scent of the animal acting like a balm. Hard to believe she'd once been so tiny that Milly could cuddle her close and sing her lullabies until the cub relaxed into a trusting, boneless sleep.

This bear had been her very first de-extinct reemerge at the Pleistocene BioPark Zoo. And when this bear hadn't taken her first breath, Milly had been the one who'd suctioned fluids from her nose and throat, puffed air into her mouth to expand lungs, heard her sharp first cries.

Milly's arms tightened over Maskwa. Not *this* bear.

Her bear.

The low hum of voices from the veterinary team, the click of metal instruments on trays as carts rolled into the surgical suite, and hiss of the oxygen cone covering Maskwa's face intertwined with the bear's heartbeat and breathing. Milly buried her face in the bear's fur one last time, but her gut refused to release its tightly coiled tension.

Nothing was ever considered routine with de-extincts, and the surgery would need to be swift for the welfare of the animal.

John Radebe, the head bear keeper, stood outside the surgical suite behind thick metal bars that made up one wall of the theater. Two long poles lay on a table behind him—*flash sticks*, he called them—the red one tipped with a syringe holding extra anesthesia, the green one with the anesthesia reversal. Close enough to inject more sedative in case the bear showed signs of premature revival.

"How you doin', Milly?" John called, his deep baritone possessing a lovely French-Senegalese accent.

"Living the dream, John."

Milly straightened and gave Maskwa one last affectionate pat. Technician at her side, dental team by Maskwa's head, and John in the observation corridor, she called, "Okay, everyone, let's do this by the book and get out of here. Better on the bear, better on us."

She pivoted to grab blue nitrile gloves, catching an unexpected face peering through the security door's observation window. Lead geneticist Dr. Luther Nikolai pierced her with his scowling gaze before he backed into the shadows.

Milly whirled her back to the door, shaking hand tucking a lock of hair behind her ear, cursing her reaction to the man. She was known for her control, her calm, secretly proud of her steadiness. And she could usually control her stupid reaction to Luther Nikolai if given a heads-up, because it was just plain *stupid* to have a stupid juvenile crush on her boss, especially after so many years working together.

She stared down at an instrument tray, unconsciously ticking off each component from a detailed mental list.

Besides, he'd apologized for the kiss. Too much celebratory vodka, he'd explained with an embarrassed grimace. A mistake.

He'd been distant ever since. *So why did he come?*

Nerves jumping, Milly snapped on her gloves and tugged her mask into place, suppressing a need to glance back at the window. Maskwa came first today. No. *Every* day. Taking a cleansing breath, she picked up a thinscreen—a slim, lightweight tablet—to scan Maskwa's body, noting a hot spot on her upper right mammary.

"I can't believe the state of these teeth." Across the bear from Milly, veterinary dentist Carin Zuanick bent her head until it practically disappeared into Maskwa's enormous open maw. "This bear has at least three moderate and I don't know how many incipient cavities, along with the rotting canine. This root canal is going to be major surgery, but now I need time to drill out and patch at least two of her other teeth. And who's fault is that, Sabrina?"

"I don't know what you're talking about, Dr. Zuanick." Sabrina Navas's voice came out weak and shaky. Carin's longtime technician, Sabrina had already been on the razor edge of Carin's tongue before the team had entered the surgical suite, and they were only five minutes into the exam.

"'I don't know what you're talking about.' You gave this bear her last dental checkup six months ago. I read the report. None of this"— Carin waved her hand sharply at the bear's head—"was in it. Why is that? Oh, I know. Pure incompetence."

"Cut it out, Carin." Milly stared at Maskwa's heart rate on the thinscreen. A little slow, but she'd had to adjust the sedation dose up because of Maskwa's fall weight gain for her upcoming hibernation. Too much drug would slow revival. Too little risked early emergence— waking up during the surgery—which could be catastrophic for everyone in the room. "We won't have time for anything but the root canal, and don't mess with her intubation tube like that." Leaning over the bear, she visually checked the line to make sure it was still in place before she picked up the battery-powered razor and shaved an area inside Maskwa's front leg for an IV.

"I can't get to her teeth with the frickin' thing in the way. What the *hell*, Sabrina?" Carin flung the dental instrument Sabrina had handed her against the theater wall. It rang with a metallic clang and clattered to the floor. "That's *not* what I asked for. How many times—"

Sabrina cowered by a tray of instruments.

"You know what? I'm sick of you and your inability to do your job. Get out." Carin leaned into Sabrina's personal space, index finger stabbing the air. "I never want to see your face again, do you understand? I'll do this myself because *you're fired.*"

With a sob, Sabrina pivoted and dashed by Milly, brushing against her. She slammed her hand against the green-lighted panel to open the security door and ran out, crying piteously.

John started after her.

"John, no," Milly said. "You have to stay. Protocol."

He gritted his teeth, his gaze pinned on the window of the security door.

"You know, John, because she's so bad at her job, I can't believe poor little Sabrina is as good at handling *your* instrument as I was." Carin smirked. "Miss me yet?"

John grabbed the bars, knuckles bloodless, jaw like iron. "Carin, you are truly a vicious—"

"Careful," she warned, not looking up from the bear's mouth. "If you call me a bitch, I'll file a hostile-work-environment and gender-bias complaint against you as fast as you can blink and make sure you're fired. How would you support your precious unemployed girlfriend then?"

John turned away with a jerky, ungraceful motion. His back to the theater, he clutched the edge of the flash-stick table, body rigid.

"Dr. Nikolai won't let you do that, Carin." Milly popped a third blood-collection tube into the sterile plastic sheath, lips pressed tight at the gratuitous drama. God *bless* it, if these people would keep it in their pants instead of hopping from one bed to another.

"He won't have a choice. When Luther and I were married, I was privy to all his secrets, some of which were quite … revealing." Unmasked—she rarely wore one—Carin Zuanick smiled smugly at the security door's window. "If he doesn't do what I want, *give* me what I want, I could just as easily wreck *his* career. Isn't that right, любимый?"

Darling. Milly pushed away a twinge of envy.

Carin grabbed the drill from the dental cart and revved it. It hummed high then whined low as she pressed it into the bear's left mandibular canine. An unpleasant shiver vibrated through Milly's spine.

"Dr. Smith?" A masked technician she didn't recognize caught her attention. Cool brown eyes with blue-gray rings around the irises stared into hers. "White count high."

Milly, pressing her fingers around Maskwa's mammaries, replied, "Not surprising with the tooth. One of her teats is a little tight and hot, too. We haven't met yet. You're on Dr. Appleton's team?" Gavin Appleton, senior vet at the BioPark, had been slated to oversee Maskwa's surgery but had been called to an emergency at the woolly rhinoceros paddock. "Please culture her blood to see if anything grows out."

"Yes, ma'am." He plucked a loaded syringe from the cart and handed it to her. "Broad spectrum antibiotic." Standard procedure for an infected tooth.

The *ma'am* stung a little—she wasn't that old—yet she smiled at him from under her mask. "Thanks." Polite, efficient. He anticipated her needs well. Maybe she could lure him away from Appleton. Milly twisted the syringe into the IV, locking it tight, and slowly plunged in the antibiotic.

"*Gah*—" Carin pulled back, the drill still whining in her hand as viscous liquid shot in a narrow stream from Maskwa's tooth. The pungent, sour stench of pus permeated the room. Carin grabbed a stack of sterile pads and mopped up the pinkish-yellow fluid, flinging the soiled wipes to the floor. Her gloved fingers pushed into Maskwa's gum. More pus squirted from the channel she'd opened into the pulp.

"Hey. The bear flinched." The unknown tech backed away from the table, pointing at Maskwa's front paw. "She *flinched*."

"John," Milly called, still pushing the antibiotic. "Did you see it? *John*." But he faced away, bending solicitously and speaking in soft tones to Sabrina. Milly pressed a hand into the bear's shoulder. The muscle tightened. The hairs on her arm prickled in alarm. "Did you numb her tooth, Carin?"

"What for? She's under general anes—"

The bear blinked a cold black eye. It rolled to stare at Carin.

She froze.

Milly unlocked the syringe with steady hands. "Revival protocol in play. Everyone out," she ordered.

The tech bumped hard into Milly as he fled the suite. She pitched into the corner of a heavy cart, the empty syringe spinning out of her fingers. Instruments rattled, and pain blossomed in her hip. The tech hit the panel, fleeing through the door. He slammed it shut behind him. The green light flipped to caution yellow.

Milly reached into the patch pocket of her scrub top for the syringe of extra anesthesia she'd drawn. Her fingers scrabbled. Gone.

Where is it?

Had it fallen out? Frantic, mouth dry, she shoved the cart to one side, scanning the floor.

A growl rumbled deep in Maskwa's chest. Milly tensed, dread swelling in her chest, deeply embedded survival instincts clamoring for her to run—

No. Panic would be fatal. Revival protocol was in play. Her training took over. *Evacuate extraneous personnel, then* … Calm settled into her.

"John? Sedation. Now."

John reached around Sabrina and grabbed a flash stick, threading it through the bars.

"*That's the green.*" The antidote, the revival drug. "Get the other one! Carin." Milly grabbed her arm. "We need to leave."

But the woman stood immobile, caught in Maskwa's glare.

The bear's body jerked as the needle from the red-pole syringe penetrated her skin. For a moment she relaxed. The beady eye, a second ago so transfixed and angry, blurred.

But in a single breath, the huge bear swung a paw the size of a platter to the vent tube down her throat. Claws as long and sharp as daggers scraped the tube out. Unsteadily, Maskwa rolled to her stomach, panting heavily. Her front paws flexed and splayed across the heavy operating platform.

Milly, tugging at Carin's arm, followed the rise of the massive shaggy head up and up. The bear swayed, but her eyes, pain-glazed, rage-filled, focused on the two women in front of her. She released a low-pitched bellow, fetid breath washing over Milly's face.

Carin unfroze. She thrust Milly away and rushed toward the exit. Milly, her attention on Maskwa, stumbled after her. The bear heaved herself to all fours, her eyes dark points in the white fur surrounding them, head dropping low. It swung to follow her movement.

Milly ran into Carin's back. Carin slapped the blinking yellow wall control, but the door didn't budge.

"*Open it!*" Carin screamed, pounding on the glass window. "Damn you, Luther. *Please!*"

Luther's face appeared, with the tech next to him. Carin crowded forward, blocking Milly's view, grabbing and twisting the handle. She rammed her shoulder into the door.

The lock clicked shut.

"*No!*" Carin wailed, hunching her shoulders and head, wrapping her arms protectively around her waist and unblocking the window and control panel. Red. It was red.

Oh, God. The door had been secured from the outside.

Luther's grim gaze caught Milly's, helplessness in his eyes. Her skin prickled with fear.

She swirled to a wall of brown fur. Maskwa, now on her hind legs, bellowed again, drowning out Milly's scream as a massive paw hit her shoulder with the force of a sledgehammer. Her feet left the ground, and she flew across the room. She slammed into the wall, pain exploding. Dazed, Milly slid to the floor, her shoulder in agony, able only to helplessly watch the scene unfolding before her.

Carin had slipped by the raging bear. She tore open an emergency panel and yanked out the Smith & Wesson 500. The weapon of last resort, their only hope.

To save themselves, they would have to sacrifice Maskwa.

Carin pointed the gun at the bear. Sorrow choked Milly. Tears burned in her eyes.

The concussion of the first shot closed down all of Milly's senses except sight. Everything was silence. Her pain evaporated.

Carin pulled the trigger over and over. Maskwa kept coming. Carin threw the emptied pistol and turned to run … but there was nowhere to go. The bear slammed into her with bared teeth and slashing claws.

Milly's eyelids drifted closed, shutting out the horror. Her muscles slackened, and she floated into a semiconscious state.

A warm snuffling touched her cheek. A heavy weight settled across her lap. With gentle fingers, she combed sticky, blood-spattered fur, the quiet hum of a lullaby sounding inside her.

CHAPTER TWO

THREE DAYS LATER

"DR. SMITH?" The motherly woman at the executive assistant's desk smiled, her pillowy jowls lifting below faintly worried eyes. "They're ready for you now. Do you need any help?"

She stood, reaching out a hand even though Milly was quite a distance away, perched on the edge of a sleek sofa in the reception area.

"Thank you, I'm fine." Milly pushed off the sofa, suppressing a wince at the ache in her shoulder and arm. The cold bead that had wedged in her chest since she'd been summoned to administration now pachinkoed down into her gut. No one had spoken to her about what had gone wrong during Maskwa's surgery, about what questions might be asked, about whether she could even answer them. She'd been left in the dark.

"Dr. Smith?" The woman's voice held a hint of urgency.

Milly forced a smile and smoothed her blouse to hide the sudden shakiness of her knees.

She'd dressed in the nicest clothes she had. Instead of one of her standard long-sleeved burnout tees, she wore a silky red top her mother had once said complemented her fair skin and dark hair, which was French braided today—a little messy because her shoulder still hurt—instead of pulled high in a ponytail. Black slacks in place of soft, faded, comfortable jeans. Milly tugged at the waistband. She'd forgotten how the button dug into her stomach. An outfit last worn, what? Six years ago? She'd had to slap out the dust.

At least her shoes were comfortable, even if they didn't really go with her look.

Once steady, she crossed to a heavy double door carved with the Pleistocene BioPark medallion—a shaggy mammoth with a raised trunk and huge curling tusks. She paused, gathered herself, and pushed into the conference room.

Diffused light shone through a wall of floor-to-ceiling windows, burnishing the polished wood of a large arrow-shaped table. Outside lay the sprawling maze of the BioPark with its turning fall foliage and snaking earth-toned piezoelectric walking paths. Distant mountains, the apexes of some already dusted with snow, formed a semicircle that merged with the cloudy sky.

People around the table rose as she walked across the floor. An immediate division was apparent. On the BioPark side, Milly picked out doctors Luther Nikolai and Gavin Appleton, each man her supervisor, depending on which hat she wore—research geneticist or veterinarian. Luther gave her a deliberate nod, his emotions veiled. Dr. Appleton fidgeted, his gaze never rising higher than her chin.

To Luther's right stood Dr. Hialeah Kingbird, the BioPark's public affairs director who did double duty as a staff physician. Well-respected with a down-to-earth reputation, Kingbird had a sun-touched but smooth face, accented with black-brown eyes and winged brows shaped like Milly's, except Kingbird's ancestral genetics traced back to the first people to cross the Beringia land bridge into North America. Only the silver threads in her straight black hair gave away her age, somewhere in her mid-forties. Rumor linked her romantically to Luther Nikolai. But rumor had linked half a dozen women to Luther since the Christmas party last year.

Not that Milly was counting.

Kingbird caught her eye and smiled reassuringly, but Milly was stopped by the icy chill in the woman's gaze. She licked her lips and hurried around the table to the only open chair on the BioPark's side, next to the zoo's lead attorney, something Washington—his given name escaped her. A pair of suited individuals—a woman and a man—rounded out the final seats. Staff lawyers. Milly, knees still shaky, sat. That appeared to be a signal for everyone around her to resume their seats.

Two plain-clothed police officers sat on the opposite side of the table. The woman, her gold shield hung around her neck on a lanyard, said, "Thank you for joining us, Dr. Smith. I'm Detective Natalia Roman of the New Mexico Bureau of Investigation." Tortoiseshell glasses covered light amber eyes, and she wore a plain blue Oxford button-down and fitted tweed jacket. If Milly had to match the detective to a de-extinct, she'd be an American cheetah: gracile, hair a silky blond, chin long and pointed. Roman's hands rested on an open leather folder, one side holding a thinscreen tablet, its stylus clipped to the top. The other side held an old-fashioned lined yellow pad and utilitarian pen. She didn't introduce the whip-thin male officer in the charcoal suit next to her.

Detective Roman tapped the thinscreen. "Milly Smith, doctor of paleogenetic veterinary medicine, PhD in genetic engineering and paleoembryology. Milly's your given name?" Roman didn't wait for an answer. "You did your PhD here at the park, but your vet degree in, er, Ya ... Yakut-sk, Siberia? Why was that? We have a perfectly good vet school just up the road in Colorado."

The hint of hostility and accusation in the detective's voice sent Milly's nervousness soaring. Had admin set her up as a scapegoat for Carin Zuanick's death? She searched out Luther, blinking in surprise when she found his whole attention on her. He held her gaze, his eyes softening as they touched on her face. He gave a tiny nod of encouragement. She drew on his calm expression.

"Yakutsk was the epicenter of de-extinction cloning and technology at the time," Milly replied. "The only school that had access to emerged Pleistocene animals. I applied and, to my surprise, received a full scholarship."

The detective drew her finger up the screen. "Thirty years old, employed at the BioPark for the last seven years. I see here you were also born in Siberia. You're Russian?" Her smile was thin.

"No. My father was American. He worked as head of maintenance in a number of American embassies and consulates in the region. When he was stationed in Siberia, he met and married my mother, who was a Russian citizen. When I was eight, he retired, and we moved back to the US."

Roman scribbled a note on the yellow pad. Then she placed the pen on top of her writing and looked up.

"How are you feeling?"

The abrupt shift in topics jolted Milly. Probably the detective's intent.

"Fine. A little bruised. I don't really need this." She lifted her arm, which the physical therapist had insisted be immobilized in a hammock sling for at least a week.

Roman touched the screen, glancing down as it brightened. "And your concussion? No more headaches? No dizziness?"

Milly shook her head, pretty sure the slight pressure behind her eyes had more to do with the tension in the room.

The lawyer, Washington, thrust out his chin, frowning. "Is this really necessary, Detective?"

Roman's expression hardened. "You kept a witness to a woman's brutal death from being questioned for three days, sir. I was just making sure the reason was legitimate."

"That sounds like you're accusing us of something, Detective Roman," Kingbird said. Even her voice was charismatic. Milly had heard she'd grown up speaking one of the Algonquin dialects and that English was her second language. "I assure you, no one has coached Dr. Smith about what to say, because there was no need. This incident, as horrible as it was, occurred because Dr. Zuanick panicked during an established protocol."

"So you've said, Dr. Kingbird. Now I'd like to hear what Dr. Smith has to say about these so-called established protocols."

Kingbird held the detective's gaze before nodding graciously, as if to give permission. Roman's jaw bunched. Milly braced herself.

"Dr. Smith. What are the steps in the revival protocol?"

Milly cleared her throat and glanced around the room, her eyes lighting briefly on Dr. Appleton. He'd developed the *A. simus* early emergence procedure. But Appleton had leaned into Washington, nodding his head to a whispered comment, and seemed to be only half listening.

"During surgery, it's everyone's responsibility to watch the de-extinct for—"

"The what?"

"The animal," Milly said. "Everyone watches the animal for anesthesia awareness or revival. It doesn't necessarily mean that the de-ext —the animal is truly coming out of sedation, but we treat it that way. If the revival protocol is called, all the staff except for the lead— usually the senior veterinarian—exits the surgical suite. The lead either dispenses extra sedation or calls for more. After the drug's been administered, they leave the room and lock the security door until it's deemed safe by team consensus to go back in and continue the procedure."

"Is this security door closed between the time the staff and the lead exit the room?"

"Yes. For safety reasons. If the animal wakes up unexpectedly, we don't want it escaping into the surrounding rooms where it could harm other members of the team or itself."

Roman nodded slowly. "And if a someone gets trapped in the room with a dangerous, uh, de-extinct, what happens?"

"They can still leave if it's safe. That call is made by whoever's manning the security door."

"And if it isn't safe for a team member to leave?"

Milly sighed inwardly. She was being led like a newborn camelops calf to a saber-toothed cat. Great.

"If they feel they are in mortal danger, the team member initiates the survival steps."

"Survival steps. And that involves…?"

"Accessing a gun sequestered in the suite and shooting to kill. A last resort to save their life."

"Are you trained to use this gun?"

"Yes. Everyone involved in the surgical team is required to drill with both live rounds and e-weapons." The e-weapons had the heft, recoil, and feel of live fire—even mimicking the flash and scent of cordite from the barrel—but expelled no projectiles. "I own and am permitted on both, but I've never used the gun outside of drills."

"As we've told you repeatedly, Detective, this is the first time anyone has ever had to use survival steps in the history of the BioPark," Washington said. "We have a spotless record."

"*Had* a spotless record," Roman countered, eyes flat. "How many revival protocols have you been involved in, Dr. Smith?"

"Twelve."

"How about Zuanick?" Roman asked.

"This would have been Dr. Zuanick's fifteenth revival," Washington replied. "She shot at the range every month, like clockwork."

Roman pressed her hands on the tabletop and leaned forward, eyes narrowing. "Then why did Dr. Zuanick shoot that bear at point-blank range with a large-caliber weapon and *miss* four out of five times?"

Milly jerked, astonishment stiffening her.

"Detective, the single bullet that hit the bear ended up enraging her more." Luther pushed a thinscreen with a heat signature of Maskwa across the table. A heavy red arrow pointed to an area around her right upper mammary that registered diffusely hot.

Milly knotted her brows. That didn't look ri—

She blinked. Her gaze pinned to Luther's face. *Was Maskwa still alive?*

He continued. "While many of our de-extincts can be unpredictable and dangerous, the short-faced bear is, to be blunt, terrifying. Even with all her training and experience, Carin uncharacteristically froze when revival was called. After she accessed the weapon, her fear and panic caused her hands to shake. One thousand pounds of enraged prehistoric bear will do that."

"Dr. Zuanick's initial inaction brought on her own death. It almost caused Dr. Smith's," Washington said. "Operator error." He tapped the table to punctuate each word.

Milly winced internally. Not for herself. But for the defense the BioPark would put forward to counter any civil suits brought by Carin Zuanick's family.

"It seems a number of your staff panicked," Roman shot back. "Dr. Smith, why didn't you exit the surgical theater once the bear revived?"

Gavin Appleton answered, shoulders rigid. "Because as lead, she's like the captain on a ship, the last one to leave *after* she's cleared all other personnel. She followed protocol, and her bravery almost cost her *her* life. But that's our Dr. Smith. By the book, never out of line. Calm. Predictable. Bor—er." Appleton cleared his throat, cheeks blooming red.

Milly scrunched her face. Calm, sure. It was her trademark. Predictable? Maybe.

Boring?

"I mean, Dr. Smith was incredibly lucky Maskwa didn't tear her to bloody shreds like—" Luther squeezed Appleton's arm, but the man forged on, studiously avoiding Milly's gaze. "My vet tech didn't panic either. As soon as he noted the bear's revival, he retreated to safety and followed protocol exactly as he should have."

"Then how about John Radebe?" Roman said. "He almost used the wrong medication."

"But was stopped by Dr. Smith's quick reaction," Kingbird said. "He switched flash sticks immediately and deployed the correct one."

Milly stared down at the tabletop, mind racing.

"Radebe's injected sedative obviously had no effect," Roman said.

"Not unusual. The bear's adrenaline had spiked. She was able to overcome any medication given, at least initially." Luther sighed. "Sedation of such a heavy animal with such a large amount of body fat is tricky, Detective. The anesthesia partitions into fat—"

"That means nothing to me." Roman's brows pinched in annoyance.

"Of course." Luther smiled. "Please let me explain. Because of the drug's chemical structure, it's absorbed by an animal's fat. This absorption decreases its effectiveness. However, the medication doesn't stay in the fat forever. It rereleases over time back into the animal's system. In a de-extinct that puts on hundreds of kilos preparing for hibernation, it's a balance for our veterinarians to draw the perfect amount of anesthesia. Dr. Smith walked a very fine line when she determined dose. Dr. Appleton has already gone over Dr. Smith's calculations and wouldn't have done anything different."

"If you don't believe me, check her work"—Appleton waved an impatient hand at Milly—"with your own experts."

Roman's expression soured. "Right. Every *expert* on these animals is employed by the Pleistocene BioPark system, so their judgment might be considered less than impartial."

"And you must take into account that Dr. Zuanick's actions during the procedure inadvertently increased the time it would take to finish the dental work on the bear," Kingbird said.

"Another point against Zuanick," Washington said, almost triumphantly. The two junior lawyers beside Milly scribbled madly with their styluses.

Even though the detective didn't move, she seemed to shrink a little in her chair. She leveled her gaze on Milly.

"Do you agree? Did Dr. Zuanick's negligence cause her death?"

All heads turned toward Milly. She squared her shoulders, stomach pinballing madly.

"I'm sorry, Detective. I'm afraid I don't remember anything."

CHAPTER THREE

THE LAWYERS FILED OUT THE DOOR OF THE CONFERENCE room, steps quick and purposeful. Appleton tapped his wrist tech, scrolled through messages on the wide clear band, and murmured something about woolly rhinos before he followed. Milly was alone with Luther Nikolai and Hialeah Kingbird.

She stared down at the old-fashioned business card and Detective Roman's handwritten note: *If you remember anything, please call.*

"You knew, didn't you?" Milly looked up at Kingbird.

"This type of amnesia is common after a head injury."

No denial, no affirmation. Not the answer Milly had expected.

"Why does the detective suspect Carin Zuanick's death was something other than an accident?"

"Because it's how their minds work. How they're trained." Impatience cut through Kingbird's answer.

Milly shifted her feet. She'd never understood Kingbird's hostility toward her. They hardly knew each other.

Kingbird extended her hand, eyes frosty. "Give me the card, Dr. Smith." It was an order. "If you do remember anything, you are to come to Dr. Nikolai or me first, not the police. Understood?"

Milly placed the detective's card in Kingbird's palm, careful not to touch skin. Kingbird crushed it and dropped her arm to her side.

"I have a debrief with the blood-thirsty lawyers about this mess in fifteen minutes and a million phone calls to make to the media and the board. If you'll excuse me."

Left in the conference room with Luther, Milly wandered over to the picture window, striving for composure that Kingbird had knocked wobbly and Luther disturbed by his mere presence. She focused on the vista laid out in front of her, drinking in the plains and surrounding mountains of the San Luis Valley. Over the last two decades, millions of acres had been purchased at a premium by the Russian oligarch who'd funded the BioPark. Years of intensive deconstruction and rewilding had returned the valley to nearly pristine wilderness—no more paved roads or ranches, no cabins in the mountains, towns and businesses obliterated or moved. Even old electric poles, train tracks—any aboveground infrastructure—had been demolished or buried, the terrain restored as if humans had never crossed the land bridge or sailed the ocean blue to colonize North America.

Except the whole concept—from the rewilding to the genetic engineering to the de-extinction of Pleistocene creatures, everything—was derived and controlled by humans, for humans. The hypocrisy and pious sanctimony were stunning. But she didn't care.

Because everything she did was about the animals.

Milly lay a hand against the cold glass. In the far distance, a herd of mammoths trickled single file into a conifer forest. She closed her eyes, picturing the wind teasing their thickening winter coats as they called to each other with rumbles too low for humans to hear.

She broke the silence: "Maskwa?"

"Alive. No decision has been made on her fate."

Milly's shoulders sagged in relief.

Luther stepped to her side, his handsome, saturnine face in profile, all sharp cheekbones and knife-blade jaw. Faint black stubble shaded his shaved head. Milly wondered if his hair was straight or curly. In the seven years they'd worked together, he'd never let it grow out.

"Would you like to see her?"

Milly nodded and followed him out of the conference room and to a discreet biometric elevator. When the door opened, he touched her elbow lightly, nodding for her to precede him. Heat zinged over her skin and settled in her belly. She stepped far enough away from him that he couldn't easily touch her again and stared blankly at the silvered walls. The elevator sank, opening on the first level of the extensive underground workings of the BioPark.

"It's a long walk. With your injuries, I've called for an aerolift." He gestured to the hover pod in the adjacent fast-pass corridor, the zoo's mammoth logo plastered on its hood and doors.

"I'd rather walk," Milly said. "Unless you don't have the time."

"I have the time. And I'm wearing comfortable shoes. Like you." He hesitated. "Your hair looks very nice today, Dr. Smith."

Milly almost gaped.

He started down the pedestrian walkway, careful, it seemed, not to touch her. The people they passed appeared to recognize her and Luther Nikolai, nodding or staring, sometimes rudely. She and Luther fell into a rhythm, their pace purposeful and brisk, neither speaking as they negotiated numerous automated security stations. He opened a double door, and Milly found herself in the laboratory wings. The familiar scent of disinfectant mixed with the sweetish odor of biofluids pumped through the artificial uteri in the incubation cubicles.

Her world.

And his.

Milly skewed a glance at Luther. He captured her eyes, his look intense. Her heart jumped, but he turned away quickly to open a door, a polite mask settling over his features.

He ushered her out of the labs and into a hallway that led to the de-extinct bear sector. Milly expected him to direct her to an elevator that accessed the surface off-exhibit enclosures. Instead, he steered her down an echoing stairwell and into an underground area she knew existed but had never visited. Older, colder, with an air of decay and disuse, the rooms and corridors had been decommissioned at least a decade ago. She frowned.

Luther said, "IT and maintenance did some quick retrofitting to digitize the manual controls. The board denied our request for funds, so a rush job on the cheap. Not everything was completed before the bear arrived. Caught between the Scylla and Charybdis, I'm afraid."

He tapped a newly installed thinscreen mounted beside a defunct keyless entry box. The lock clicked and the door opened into a large cement chamber containing an observation hallway with a waist-high fence that surrounded a semicircular cage. Inside the cage, water dribbled into a stained metal tub bolted to the back wall. Next to the water source, a sliding panel door allowed the animal access to an off-exhibit sleeping and feeding enclosure. The keeper's entrance to the off-exhibit area was through a door on the left-hand side of the observation hallway. Directly beside that door was a large lever once used to raise and lower the sliding panel inside the cage.

The whole ugly setup resembled the cell-like confinement used by zoos in the last century: cold, sterile, soulless.

Luther touched a second thinscreen just inside the room. The panel door inside the cage slid closed.

Milly pushed past Luther and detangled her arm from the sling. She clutched the top rail of the waist-high fence that acted as a distance barrier to the heavily barred enclosure, body quivering with outrage. The putrid stench of infection, stool, and urine blended sickeningly, a punch to her senses.

Maskwa stood on all fours in the center of the cage, head down, fur matted with feces and rotting food. She swayed back and forth, back and forth, pressing one forepaw in the cement, then the other in a rhythmic rocking. Her mouth hung slack, dripping cloudy drool in a pool below her jaw, the gum around her damaged canine angry and swollen. Dull eyes stared past Milly, no recognition in their depths. Maskwa was an animal who'd given up.

Milly whirled on Luther. *"How could you?"*

He stared down at her, brows raised as if startled by her passion.

Her own lips parted in shock … at herself.

"We tried to place her in an off-exhibit enclosure at the surface, but she could hear her cubs," he said, glancing over her shoulder. "She almost broke free. Even here, she—"

He tensed, latched his arms around Milly's waist and slung her away from the cage as Maskwa slammed her body against the bars. A powerful foreleg tipped with vicious claws raked the air where Milly had just stood.

The foreleg from the side with the bullet wound. *She isn't favoring her damaged side.*

Luther sandwiched Milly against the cinderblock wall. She clutched his heavy biceps, blinking over his shoulder at Maskwa, who again stood and rocked.

A rush of images flash-flooded Milly's memory. Her body went taut. She lifted her face to his. Luther's eyes flared.

"Are you hurt?"

"No. I remember something. You were there. At Maskwa's surgery. And you were upset. Even angry. Why?"

His fingers bit into her upper arms. Pain blossomed, and Milly cried out. He dropped his hands as if she'd burned him. The anger and distress she remembered from that day returned.

"Because you could have been killed. Because I would have lost..." He lifted his hands as if to touch her again. "Dammit, Milly. *You weren't supposed to be there.*"

CHAPTER FOUR

THE SPIKE OF ADRENALINE AND LUTHER'S NEARNESS scrambled Milly's brain, fresh and astonishing alarms ringing in her ears.

"What do you mean I wasn't supposed to be there? You would have lost … *what?*"

His expression blanked.

"What do you mean?" she pressed, flattening her palms against his chest. His heart beat like a drum.

He stepped back and rubbed both palms over his shaved head. "I meant that Appleton was scheduled, not you. I arrived at the surgical suite and saw you in his place and was surprised that the surgery was going forward. Protocol dictates cancellation and rescheduling."

She waited, nerves stretched, for his answer to her second question. What would he have lost? *Her?* But he looked away, and the hope that had ignited in her chest extinguished. Milly lifted her chin, masking her pointless hurt.

"Protocol dictates cancellation and rescheduling for routine checkups. This was not routine because of the rotten tooth. Besides, you know Dr. Appleton avoids Maskwa ever since…" Milly's face burned hot, embarrassed for her veterinary supervisor.

"Then he should avoid fluids before or wear a-a..." Luther waved a hand in the direction of his trousers, but his cheeks ruddied, too.

"Why were you there?" she asked. "You don't come to these anymore."

It wasn't an accusation, but at the same time was. He'd once been present at every checkup and surgery when the original cohort of laboratory-emerged animals were young. But as more de-extincts were successfully produced, his teams became specialized and competent. His time was now taken up with polygenetic screening, AI analysis, and de-extinction selection criteria. The overwhelming success of the two Pleistocene BioParks, this one in the US and the original in Siberia, sparked a clambering from all sides: zoological societies requesting their own woolly mammoths or saber-toothed cats as revenue boosters. Environmentalists insisting these animals should only be used as living tools to slow warming progression in tundra and taiga-rich areas of the planet. Hunters offering obscene sums of coin for trophy de-extincts. Animal-rights zealots contending the work Luther Nikolai and others at the zoo were doing was immoral, that the creatures produced had had their time on earth, that people like Luther and Milly were opening a Pandora's box: the *Jurassic Park*–Crichton Conundrum come to fruition.

And what was next? Milly had heard rumors that discussions were underway to attempt the emerging of extinct human ancestors, like the forest-dwelling *Ardipithecus ramidus* who lived over four million years ago and *Australopithecus africanus*, a member of the human family tree three million years ago with mixed ape and human characteristics. Even *Homo* species—*erectus* and *neanderthalensis*—were being whispered about, raising immensely thorny ethical issues. How would they be housed and treated? As animals or as humans?

And would it eventually lead to human cloning, forbidden now by international law?

"I was at the surgery because I had a meeting directly after with Carin."

Grief wavered over his features.

Her own anger melted. She placed a hand on his arm. "I'm sorry."

It was easy to forget Luther and Carin had been married before they'd been assigned to this BioPark, that he'd lost someone he'd once loved. They'd both moved on so completely, both linked with so many others romantically over the years. And Carin had just broken off her affair with John Radebe.

A wisp of a memory tickled Milly's mind. Carin's sly glance through the observation window. *Luther's secrets.*

"I don't blame Maskwa." Luther gestured toward the cage. "She was only doing what a bear does. I've argued against euthanasia, but I'm only one voice."

"*What?* No. That can't happen."

He sighed. "It's not final yet. The board will meet at the end of the week to make the decision."

Including today, five days. Maskwa might only have five days to live. Milly stared at the rocking bear, hand pressed tightly against her mouth. Her bear. *If she even lasts that long.*

"The infection will kill her first. She needs surgery today—at the latest tomorrow—to deal with her tooth." Milly paused. "And her bullet wound."

She watched him carefully. He wouldn't meet her eyes.

"The initial decision of the board was if they did vote for euthanasia, there would be no need to put anyone else in danger performing an unnecessary surgery."

Milly couldn't believe what she was hearing.

"You can't do that! It's *cruel* to leave her like this. It's—it's *inhuman.* We've got to fight them on this. She's in such misery; she's given up."

"So much so that she almost killed you a few minutes ago. You shouldn't have been at that surgery. I shouldn't have brought you here. You need to avoid—" Expression tight, he released a sharp breath.

"Avoid my job? Avoid danger? Why? Because I'm a woman?"

"No," Luther barked. "Because—" He clenched his jaw and fists.

Milly narrowed her eyes. This wasn't about protocols or rescheduling. Luther Nikolai had been angry that she'd been at the surgery as if … *as if he knew something bad would happen.*

In the silence, every one of Maskwa's labored breaths hit Milly like a blow. Any remaining calm, composure—*control*—deserted her.

She flung a hand toward Maskwa. "You used to come to these surgeries because you said these creatures were like your children. You came to watch over them, to insist they be treated with kindness and compassion. I admired that man. He was my idol. What happened to him?"

His jaw tightened until it resembled steel. "There comes a time when what is needed is for someone to step back and see the whole picture. You have the luxury of focusing on details—"

"*Maskwa is not a detail*. She's a living, breathing creature we brought back by force to a world that eliminated her kind long ago. She has only us." Milly rubbed her brow, a plan forming. "I just want to relieve her pain. Give me permission for another surgery. I can do this. I can save—"

"No, Milly." Luther held out his hands in supplication. "Please understand, I would do everything I could to shield you from harm. But I won't be able to protect you if you interfere in these matters. The board will fire you."

If she lost her job, she'd lose her ability to help the de-extincts.

This career was her life. Everything she'd trained for. All her studies were for one purpose: to resurrect that which had been lost forever. To defeat extinction. That meant every creature—every life—at the BioPark mattered.

Maybe the board would vote to let Maskwa live. But she wouldn't get that chance if she died from something as easily fixed as an infected tooth.

Milly lifted her chin. "This isn't about me. If you won't fight for Maskwa, I will."

"*Don't even think*—" Face red, Luther stabbed a finger in her face. "You stay away from that bear and this investigation. That's an order, Dr. Smith."

Scowling, he touched the thinscreen. The door clicked open. He took Milly by the elbow and escorted her from the room. As the door closed behind them, the last thing Milly saw was the bear's confused, pain-filled eyes.

She jerked away from Luther and strode down the hallway. She'd helped bring this creature back into a world that had left her far behind. The de-extincts were Milly's responsibility, her genetic children, too, something Luther had taught her. Something he seemed to have forgotten.

A quick glance behind her showed him heading away from her, back hunched, hands shoved into his pockets. Luther Nikolai was hiding something.

Orders be damned. Milly pivoted around a corner and made a beeline for the surgical suite where Carin Zuanick had died so horribly. She needed answers to why the first surgery had gone so wrong, and she *refused* to let the bear suffer. Which meant she had questions to ask—and a clandestine surgery to plan that night.

CHAPTER FIVE

NOT WANTING TO ALERT SECURITY OR LUTHER TO HER movements, Milly snagged Gavin Appleton's extra biometric security fob to open the door to surgical suite 15-A. Notorious for shortcuts, the head vet left one hidden in the first aid kit for his trusted techs. Saved him time for more important things, he said, and gave them prep experience. Strange that it was still there after the investigation into Carin Zuanick's death, but Milly didn't question her luck.

Motion-triggered lights flickered on as she entered the observation corridor surrounding the surgical suite. Once inside the suite, Milly turned on the light then slowly rotated in place. Her gaze touched the huge center platform, the barred area of wall behind which John Radebe would stand with his flash sticks, and the empty panel that housed the gun Carin had used to shoot Maskwa. The suite was so clean, the BioPark board could hold a dinner fundraiser on the instrument gurneys if not the floor.

Milly slipped on protective glasses, turned off the lights, and switched on a handheld ultraviolet lamp. She started a slow, painstaking journey around the lab. It would be easier if she watched the recorded CCTV footage of the surgery, but right now she didn't want her memories force-fed to her by the single godlike ceiling camera. She wanted the details. Her own impressions of the event, her own emotions, her own fear and terror and pain—if she could retrieve them from the fog of amnesia.

A smeared spatter fluoresced electric blue on the floor at the head of the huge platform. She stared at it with knotted brows. The hum of a drill, and a putrid slap of odor. Carin's isolated figure, gloved hand reaching into Maskwa's mouth, pressing, pus spurting.

Then nothing as murk rolled back to obscure.

She replayed the memory, her image of Carin standing at Maska's head somehow amiss.

Milly scuttled to where she would've been standing and closed her eyes. The IV placed in Maskwa's left foreleg, the blood drawn, flushing the line, and setting the T and male adapter.

She frowned, exasperated with herself. She was creating a memory based on past surgeries, and immediate emotion was interfering—

Exasperation. She inhaled sharply. Not interfering. Her immediate emotion *reflected the event.* She wasn't annoyed with herself but with the others in the suite. With Carin and Sabrina Navas, Carin's dental technician. And worried. About what? She pulled back her memory of Carin standing alone over Maskwa's head.

Where was Sabrina? The two women had worked as a team during the years Milly had been on staff, and had been friends, then enemies, then back again more times than Milly could count. Enemies now because of John Radebe. Because Carin had been replaced in his affections by Sabrina. And the jealousy that animated the women's recent relationship was corrosive.

Remembrance rose like a bubble through molasses—a metal instrument flung in anger against the far wall. From behind the platform, Milly stared at a shadowed region of the floor. Not one instrument. Three dental tools had lain silvery in the bright overhead light. One could be labeled as a mistake or incompetence. But *three ...*

You must take into account Dr. Zuanick's actions.

Carin had fired Sabrina Navas on the spot.

Had Carin found a convenient way to get rid of her rival?

Or had Sabrina deliberately pricked at Carin's mercurial temper until it burst? Had she set up her boss's murder with no care for anyone else in the room?

Murder?

Where had that come from? Milly shook the thought from her head. The scenario was too random and inefficient. Besides, as surgical lead, Milly herself would have been the last person to leave the room. No way Sabrina could've known Carin would be trapped with an enraged animal.

This couldn't be what Luther was hiding anyway since everything captured on video had been openly discussed at the meeting this morning.

What was she still missing? Frustration swelled at the blankness of her mind.

Milly shook it off and refocused on what was important: Maskwa, in pain and with the threat of euthanasia hanging over her head. Besides, Milly's memory was coming back, even if it was piecemeal. Like recovering from sedation and playing out her own revival protocol. She swept the light across the floor, continuing her search.

Against the wall farthest from the security door, the UV light picked up an area with an overwhelming glow, as if the room had absorbed such terror and agony, no amount of scrubbing could ever wash it away. This had to be where Carin Zuanick died.

Staring at the spot retrieved no memories and evoked only sadness. Milly turned and followed the UV-bright smears of serum across the room to the cage bars that fronted John Radebe's observation post. An exit sign around the corner illuminated the hallway table a macabre red, like it was washed with blood. Milly tucked the UV light in her pocket and grasped the bars to stare at the table, layering what she knew over what she couldn't remember.

John always carried two long jab sticks with automatic syringes: a red one filled with a powerful opioid sedative specifically designed for large de-extincts, the green stick tipped with Narcan antidote. Because a tiny amount of the sedative was lethal in humans, the syringes were purchased predrawn to decrease the possibility of accidental exposure and were easily attached to the head of the flash sticks. Of course, that also made them easy to detach. Two syringes, clearly labeled, so John couldn't have mixed them up.

Could he? Milly nibbled her lip.

Detective Roman had said John had used the red stick to deliver more sedative but that Maskwa hadn't responded. Milly had seen animals react that way before, both at the BioPark and in the wild. If asked, her reply to why the backup sedative hadn't worked would have been the exact same as Luther's—a surge of adrenaline.

That's why the gun was the last resort.

Even that method was tenuous. A kill shot would be almost impossible with the level of fear and panic Carin must have felt. But that she'd missed the massive bear four out of five times in such a small space was scarcely credible.

Milly switched on the lights again. She positioned herself next to the empty gun panel and drew an imaginary weapon. Clasping her hands, she pointed her index fingers up at the mirage of a bear rising to its back legs. She retreated to where Carin had awaited death, pretend firing five times. Her imagination soared and filled the quiet space with the boom of shots and shrill screams.

Milly unclasped trembling hands. How much worse would it have been for Carin? Firearms training taught her that tiny movements— the pulse of a heartbeat or a jerk in anticipation of the recoil—could affect the placement of a shot by centimeters, if not meters, at a distance.

She hurried across the room to count the bullet gouges inside the suite, finding three deeply spalled impact craters in the cement wall. Where was the fourth hole? She touched the gouges one by one, hand trailing toward the security door.

Her breath caught. Centered at chest level, one bullet had punched a hole completely through the reinforced metal security door. Ridiculously dangerous to anyone lingering in the observation corridor.

She'd missed it completely when entering the suite. And no wonder. The black frame that surrounded the window had obscured it.

But nothing definitively proved Luther Nikolai had hidden information or outright lied to her.

Yet.

Milly turned off the lights and slipped out of the surgical suite. She had more questions now than before and needed someone to answer them. But she still had to recruit her team for Maskwa's surgery that evening.

If her luck held, she knew someone who could do both.

CHAPTER SIX

MILLY STRODE UP THE PATH TO THE OFF-EXHIBIT WOOLLY rhino pens, feeling more like herself after detouring to her on-site condo and changing into jeans and a long-sleeved tee. Hands tucked into the pockets of a drab green puffy jacket, her eyes traced the robust lines of the stocky woollies, the odd cinnamon-and-beige barber-pole striping of their nose horns and almost comical shortness of their legs. Their earthy bovine scent swept past in a gentle rush of wind, and the female, Freya, cocked an eye in Milly's direction. A foot stomped in warning, prompting Balder to snuggle closer to his mate.

Dr. Gavin Appleton leaned against the fortified fence of pipe and steel cable, dressed in a dark blue scrub top with a waffled Henley underneath against the chill. He glanced at his wrist tech but didn't turn to address her, instead keeping his face and body in profile. "You're eight minutes late."

He had to raise his voice to be heard over the humming drills, banging hammers, and the steady beeps of heavy equipment that sounded in the distance, work proceeding on the brand-new woolly rhinoceros exhibit. To celebrate its opening, the BioPark board had planned a huge black-tie event.

"Sorry, sir. How's Freya doing? Any lingering effects?"

Appleton shrugged his age-thickened, rounded shoulders. "Nothing. Nothing at all. I'm beginning to think she didn't really eat that plastic bag. That all that happened was some intern forgot to log it in as disposed of and a keeper panicked, thus an anonymous text on the emergency thread. Covered their asses by hitting the panic button." He shifted to rub a hand over his stubbled jaw. "Or, at worst, a prank that resulted in a waste of my time and sleep deprivation."

There was both relief and ire in his voice. Relief because losing Freya would put the BioPark back years on the woolly rhino breeding program. And ire because, from what Milly had heard, Appleton had spent countless hours at the woolly rhino enclosure, prepped for emergency surgery.

Did those hours ease his guilt for abandoning Maskwa's surgery three nights earlier? Would Carin Zuanick have died so horribly if he'd stayed?

"The bag could still be hung up in her gut, but with the amount of excrement that animal's produced in the last three days…" He shook his head, his attention focused on the rhinos.

Appleton was thirty years older than Milly, and his experience with de-extinct creatures was legendary. He knew more about these animals and how they worked than anyone on earth. He'd come in on the ground floor with the San Luis Valley BioPark and had a hand in caring for nearly every de-extinct produced, whether lab emerged or by natural birth. But he was personally invested in the woolly and hovered over them like a mother hen. She'd heard it was because he'd been present during the death of the last remaining white rhino so had a soft spot for rhinos of any kind.

Which probably answered her next question. She weighed her words carefully.

"Sir? I was the on-call vet the day of Maskwa's surgery. I've checked my messages. I received nothing about the woolly rhino emergency. Only your text summoning me to replace you."

Appleton's body swelled as he drew a long breath. "It seems I was the only one who received that call. Whoever reported must have known the woollies are special to me, just as that bear is to you."

Good answer. Still …

She pushed harder. "You were scrubbed and prepped for Maskwa's surgery."

"You mean I should have stayed instead of calling you in." He slanted her a glance then shook his head. "Look at the big picture, Dr. Smith. I'm the only vet who could absorb the blowback if something happened to Freya or Balder. I made a command decision, and I stand by it. No matter what Luther Nikolai says, Carin's death was a tragic accident."

Milly straightened. "Dr. Nikolai didn't approve?"

Appleton waved a dismissive hand, profile grumpy. "I was better for the rhino. He knows that. You were better for the bear. Maybe I should've waited until you arrived, but time was of the essence."

Appleton had his quirks: his incontinence when working with large carnivorous cats and bears, his borderline obsession with time. But did he count the minutes because, more and more, he lost them to a worrying forgetfulness? The other techs and vets—even Milly— covered for him, his knowledge and experience a valuable commodity no one wanted to waste. But how long before he became a real danger to himself and everyone around him?

"Why did you place me as lead in Maskwa's surgery?" Milly asked.

Milly and Appleton had worked together for five years, but they'd never gotten close. That was fine with her. She preferred a professional relationship and the boundaries that came with it, even if her emotions played traitor around Luther Nikolai. To Appleton's credit, he never held back his knowledge or played favorites.

"That's just it," he said gruffly. "I didn't give you lead, at least not that I—" He cleared his throat.

Recall, Milly inserted silently.

"Carin Zuanick was the obvious lead because she attended all the pre-op briefings and has—had—more experience." Another sidelong glance. "I'm not sure why you changed it."

"I changed myself to lead?" That didn't sound like her. "Did Dr. Zuanick know?"

"Surely you would have told her." A chill breeze teased Freya's fur, revealing the woolly undercoat.

"When we were in with the police this morning—"

His hands tightened on the railing, knuckles white. "I didn't tell them about the switch on advice of counsel. I'd been informed about your amnesia, and it was decided it would be easier."

"You knew about my amnesia."

He shifted and swallowed hard. If the man had a handkerchief, he'd be dabbing his brow.

"But what if I had remembered?" she said.

"Not possible."

Milly opened her mouth to argue, to tell him her memory was creeping back, then snapped it shut. The hair on her neck stood.

How can he be so sure?

"Anything else? I'm due at the yeti enclosure in"—he consulted his wrist tech—"thirteen minutes." By yeti, he meant the *Gigantopithecus blacki*, the huge de-extinct great ape that measured ten feet tall in a bipedal stance. Cryptozoologists swore they were the explanation for Bigfoot. "Looks like Elizabeth Barrett may finally be pregnant by Robert Browning."

The unofficial names given to individuals in the *G. blacki* troop were that of nineteenth century authors and poets.

"Just one more thing." Milly hesitated.

"About Maskwa?" He finally met her eyes and forced an indulgent smile. "First time you've had to deal with juried euthanasia, isn't it?" He bobbed his head. "I know, I know. The bear was just being a bear. But we aren't in a position to ignore that people are in daily contact with this very dangerous de-extinct. The BioPark board will give all sides a fair hearing. Frankly, it would be easier if the bear succumbed to her injuries, but Nikolai..." His spiel ended on a mutter.

So much for asking Appleton for help with Maskwa's surgery. Luckily, she'd planned for noes.

"The technician assisting that day. The one who first noticed Maskwa's revival. Does he feel the same way?"

For the first time in the conversation, Appleton's eyes brightened.

"Doyle Amon? Not at all. He's devastated. You know, he trained at the original Pleistocene BioPark in Siberia. Good man. Came highly recommended. Seems to know what I need during procedures before I do." He grinned. "He's not as bor—er, I mean he's not as by the book as you are, Dr. Smith, but he'll learn."

Boring. Milly blinked at her spike of irritation. He'd said the same thing at the meeting that morning. Was this how her colleagues thought of her? "I'd like to speak to him about the surgery."

Appleton's smile disappeared. "Why?"

"For his impressions on what happened."

"If you want to know what happened, watch the CCTV of the surgery. Nikolai or Kingbird will send you the link. They had it scrubbed off the system, of course." Appleton checked the time again. "The board didn't want anyone to release or sell it. Amazing what people will do for coin nowadays." He tapped his wrist tech. "Seven, no, six minutes. I need to go." Appleton turned away again and marched off. Milly hurried after him.

"I'll watch it eventually. But right now, I'm trying not to create false visual memories. It's easy to do with retrograde amnesia. That's why I'd like to talk to Mr. Amon first."

Appleton stopped beside his personal EV-Amphibious 8x8 and scratched his chin.

"I guess it couldn't hurt." It sounded like he was trying to convince himself. He climbed into the driver's seat and tapped his wrist tech. "Doyle's tracking app has him in my lab. There's a pile of blood samples from the sabers and Am-lions he's processing for SARS-CoV-2 and feline leukemia virus. Just precautionary. I'll text and tell him you're on your way." Appleton pushed the start button, and the eight-wheeled XTV hummed on. "Dr. Smith, there's, uh, something else you need to know." He stared at his hands clasped around the vehicle's wheel, face the color of bricks. "Apparently, I made an error on the initial calculations for the bear's sedation. The amount wouldn't have been enough to keep Maskwa asleep for the allotted time. You, uh, caught it."

In keeping with what he and Luther had told the detective—that

Milly had measured out an appropriate dose. Except he'd left out his own mistake.

"You must have been distracted by the woolly emergency, sir," she replied. "Maskwa still revived early."

"Yes, but I don't distinctly remember drawing ... I thought my tech..." Troubling confusion passed over his face. "It doesn't matter. What's done is done."

Frowning, Milly watched as he drove off.

Why had she changed herself to lead, especially when she was junior to Carin Zuanick? Why had the BioPark kept that information from the police? And why was Appleton so certain her amnesia wouldn't clear?

Milly tucked her questions away for the moment. She didn't want them to distract from recruiting a team to relieve Maskwa's pain, that evening, if possible. Her immediate focus would be Appleton's new tech, Doyle Amon. She didn't remember him, but Appleton's affirmative response had sparked her own positive internal reaction. Hopefully, Amon would be receptive to her extremely desperate request to help with the surgery—and flattered enough when she asked that he'd answer her questions.

Or at least wouldn't report her to Luther Nikolai.

With one last glance at the dozing pair of woollies, Milly skipped to the nearest underground access and Appleton's lab to find Doyle Amon.

CHAPTER SEVEN

APPLETON'S LAB WAS EMPTY, BUT THE BENCHTOP BLOOD analyzer was running. Milly did a quick check of the thinscreen by the door.

At the Doline Café for coffee. Put the blood samples on my bench. D. Amon

Milly, who was feeling a little peckish herself, headed to the coffee shop.

The Doline Café, one of a half dozen staff-only subterranean restaurants, spilled out from underground into a large round open-air patio with natural rock walls reaching up thirty feet to the surface. A variety of de-extinct flowering plants lovingly tended by the BioPark's Horticultural Genetics staff dotted the rock shelves. Milly made a mental note to stop by the hort-gen lab after Yukie came back from her expedition and request more *stenophylla* for her balcony flower box. Maybe ask her best friend if she'd like to drive down to Santa Fe for a girl's night out or go on a hike or a climb and ... talk.

As the only children of older parents, she and Yukie had bonded in the first year of their PhD program at the BioPark, even though Yukie teasingly referred to their personalities as "water and champagne." A compliment, she'd insisted with her infectious laugh, because even though champagne was fun while it lasted, cool, clear water quenched a thirst that sustained life, especially this life they'd created at the BioPark.

Yukie knew all of Milly's secrets, including her crush on Luther Nikolai that had been exposed by a single Christmas kiss. The one party where Milly had drowned her embarrassment in too many drinks. The one party where Yukie had helped her home instead of the other way around. Where Yukie had put *her* to bed and sat with *her* while she cried. *A mistake. My apologies.*

And Milly knew all of Yukie's secrets, even why Yukie lived life like every day was her last.

She pushed through the double glass doors, her mind busy making detailed lists of necessities for Maskwa's surgery. She tapped in her order of an apple-berry pastry—triple the price of the synthed ones that harbored an underlying taste of the fungi-based matrix—and a surprisingly rich synthed Kona coffee. She asked the cashier if Amon was in the café. The woman pointed to a man sitting at a wrought-iron table on the patio, back against the rock wall. He was staring at her.

Milly held his gaze, suppressing a squiggle of disappointment, and nodded in greeting. She didn't remember him. He stood when she reached the table.

"Dr. Smith." His voice contained wary surprise expressed in a nasal accent she recognized from her time in Siberia. "Won't you sit down?"

Doyle Amon stepped around the table, sinewed forearms flexing as he deftly pulled out one of the heavy iron-work chairs, his skin tanned from outdoor exposure. Beneath his powder-blue scrubs, he had the hard body of a runner or hiker, someone who was never still, always roaming, like a *Canis latrans* or *lupus*. His face was pleasant, features blunt. Easily forgettable, except for his eyes—blue gray with dark limbal rings surrounding the irises. He sat and folded callused hands on the table. Her thumb ran over similar spots on her own palm. She added rock climbing to his repertoire.

"I'm sorry for interrupting your break, but Dr. Appleton said he texted you I was coming?"

Amon grabbed his bare wrist and grimaced. "Sorry. I left my band in lab. Not fond of that tracking app. Makes me feel like a rewilded de-extinct whose every move is monitored. Dr. Appleton insists on it, but I only wear it when he's around."

Milly nodded in understanding. She'd deleted the tracking app from her tech the minute her rotation with Appleton had ended.

"Mr. Amon. I'd like to ask you a few questions about the events that led to Dr. Zuanick's death."

He sat up straighter, shoulders stiff. "The police and BioPark's lawyers have already done that. I filed my statement."

"This is off the record. I have no memory of what happened—a retrograde amnesia, I'm afraid—and would like to fill in the blanks."

Amon's brows lifted. "Amnesia?" He studied her, his gaze dropping to her sling. "All right."

"Did you and I speak before the surgery?"

"No time. Navas and I were setting up the trays, and Maskwa was already in the dumbwaiter, ready for anesthesia. We were maybe ten, fifteen minutes from lowering it into the suite when Dr. Appleton got the woolly rhino call, and everything stopped until you came and took over."

Dumbwaiter was the nickname for the boxy cages built above surgical suites. Hydraulics lowered them into the room after the de-extinct was sedated. Once the animal was deemed safe, the barred sides and top were raised, leaving the platformed floor as the surgical table. It was genius.

Unless the animal woke up and climbed off.

"Dr. Appleton said he was glad you were the vet on call," Amon said. "I also heard you adjusted Maskwa's sedation dose. The old man's losing it, you know? By the time you were scrubbed, Maskwa was already in the suite, ready to go, just like me." He stared down at his coffee. "I was asked not to mention that to the police—that we hadn't coordinated as a team before surgery. They—Appleton and brass—said that the fact he met with you was enough to fulfill the SOP."

But Appleton said he'd left before she had arrived. Another small omittance by the BioPark.

"Tell me about the surgery," Milly said.

He outlined it step by step, rolling his eyes when he talked about Carin firing Sabrina. "Dr. Zuanick said Navas handed her the wrong instrument three times in a row. It just didn't make sense. Navas is a licensed veterinarian in Mexico, just couldn't pass the US exam. English as a second language, you know?"

Milly nodded. The instruments part jibed with her memory flash. "Why was the revival protocol invoked?"

"Maskwa flexed her paw. I'd seen revival a few times during *A. simus* surgery in Siberia. They're notorious for it, especially when they're in their hyperphagia phase. I followed procedure and evacuated. I didn't expect what happened with Dr. Zuanick, that she would freeze like that. You were brave to stay in there. Then when Dr. Nikolai refused to open the door and let you out..."

Luther wouldn't open the door? "You were there?"

"Right next to him. I saw Maskwa knock you away." His face was pained. "After that, the whole place went crazy. Nikolai ran to the other side with Radebe and Navas. He loaded and used the backup dose of sedative on Maskwa, not that it helped. Well, Zuanick, I mean. It helped you. You were lying up against the wall. At first, I thought you were dead, too, but when Maskwa put her head on your lap, you started stroking her and humming."

Milly dug for that memory but came up with nothing.

"You were at the observation window the whole time?" At his nod, she asked, "Did you see Dr. Zuanick shoot Maskwa?"

"Yeah." He shook his head. "I was shocked the bear lived with all those gunshot wounds."

"Dr. Zuanick missed four out of five times. The surgical suite is shot to pieces."

Including the bullet hole through the metal door, right where he said he'd been standing when Carin fired the gun.

His brows slammed together. "What?"

"It was pure luck no one in the observation corridor was killed."

Amon frowned into his coffee, his hand tightening on the mug.

"What happened after?" Milly asked. He seemed lost in thought. "Mr. Amon?"

"Sorry. We were all pretty shaken up, but Navas was hysterical. Screaming and crying. Complete meltdown. You'd have thought she was responsible. Radebe and Nikolai took over. Back to protocol with a vengeance. Cleared us from observation and sent us to the presurgical conference room to wait. Told us not to discuss anything with each other until security came and got us for statements."

"Have you been back to the surgical suite?"

"No."

"And you haven't watched the closed-circuit video of the surgery?" Milly asked.

He barked out a laugh. "Are you kidding? They scrubbed that off the system as part of cleanup." Amon shook his head sadly. "Poor Maskwa. And Dr. Zuanick, of course. But I don't fault Maskwa. She was a bear being a bear. She's alive, then?"

Amon's final statement was enough for Milly to make up her mind about including him in her scheme.

"The board is taking a few days to determine her fate, but she's still in terrible pain from a bullet wound and her tooth." She clasped her hands, lacing her fingers. "I came to ask you something important. You can say no, but I'd like your word that you'll keep this to yourself, at least until it's over."

At his cautious nod, Milly leaned toward him. "I want to finish what we started with Maskwa—complete her surgery—but this will be without authorization." She explained her plan, keeping her voice low.

Amon sat back in his chair when she was done.

"A second chance. Sure," he said. "I'm in."

Milly stood. "I'll contact you with a time and the location. It might be late."

"Do you need any help setting up?" He stood, too.

"Maybe. I'll text you instructions. But you need to know that *this* surgery will be by the book, even if I don't have permission."

"Sometimes it's better to ask forgiveness than permission," Amon said with a slight smile.

She turned to leave and paused. "One more thing. Do you know of anyone who might have wanted to harm Carin Zuanick?"

Amon snorted. "I can think of three right off the top of my head. Luther Nikolai. From what I heard at the surgery, it sounded like she was on the cusp of blackmailing him with 'secrets.'" He crooked his fingers into air quotes. "Sabrina Navas. I've only been here a few weeks, but it was easy to see she and Dr. Zuanick hated each other. And John Radebe. I heard that he and Zuanick had a relationship that exploded with more force than 5A plastic because he hooked up with Navas. Why? Do you think this whole mess wasn't an accident?"

Milly wasn't ready to answer that question. Nor ask him more of her own: *What about you? Did you have a reason to harm Carin Zuanick?* She didn't want to alienate him now that he'd agreed to help her.

When she didn't respond, he stood. "I need to get back. I'll make sure to keep my wrist tech on me for your text. And thanks for trusting me enough to do this. See you soon, I guess." He left, pushing through the cafe doors and disappearing down the hall.

Feeling a little less pressure now that she'd recruited the first member of her team, Milly finished her coffee and pastry, rerunning the conversation. Amon had called admin *brass*. And 5A plastic—PVV 5A plastic—was the Russian equivalent of a military-grade C-4 explosive she'd seen used to clear away boulders for an exhibit at the Siberian Pleistocene facility. Doyle Amon might be a veterinarian technician and a hiker and a rock climber. But she'd also bet he'd been one other thing in his life—a Russian soldier.

One other thing was clear: either Amon was lying about where he'd stood during Maskwa's attack …

Or something was off with the gun.

CHAPTER EIGHT

MILLY SEARCHED FOR JOHN RADEBE AROUND THE DE-extinct bear grotto, a beautiful, forested setting filled with fragrant evergreens, gnarled oaks, and stands of white-barked aspen, their shimmering leaves gold with fall. She combed both public and behind-the-scenes enclosures and houses, including those for the short-faced bear like Maskwa and her half-grown twin cubs, and the cave bear, *Ursus spelaeus*. A single specimen, although two more were in the 3D uterine incubation rooms, ready to be emerged in the depths of winter. The family of African Atlas bear, *Ursus arctos crowther*, enter-tained the crowd, playing with enrichment—pumpkins stuffed with apple and nut butter. Their enclosure included a detailed trompe l'oeil mural of the Roman Colosseum, a reminder that this bear had been used by the Roman Empire in its *damnatio ad bestias* public executions. Ironic that the de-extinct Atlas bears turned out to be vegetarian.

She didn't find John.

Not wanting to call or text and leave evidence that could be used against them if they were caught—that is, if John would even agree to help her with Maskwa's clandestine surgery—she finally decided to ask one of his assistant keepers where he was.

Milly found a keeper in the bear grotto's kitchen, chopping up huge pieces of raw red meat into fist-sized chunks. The BioPark supplemented the synthed protein fed to the carnivores by purchasing refrigerator trucks full of locally sourced beef and bison. Keepers of carnivorous de-extincts swore the taste of real blood and the crunch of bone placated the animals, suppressing their need to hunt and kill and making them safer. Milly wasn't so sure about that, but no doubt the keepers supplemented their own kitchen pantries with select cuts of meat otherwise unaffordable to the average BioPark worker.

"As far as I know, he's at home," the keeper said and raised the cleaver. *Thwack.* Blood splattered her white paper apron. "Word is he took a few days' bereavement leave"—massive eye roll—"after Dr. Zuanick's death. Like anyone believes that. Hey, look at this." She held up a slab of meat. In the center was a dark, ragged indentation. "A bullet hole. Weird." She flipped the meat over and grimaced at the mangled damage to the raw flesh, then dropped it on the cutting surface. *Thwack.* "The day before Zuanick was killed, she was at the grotto, and she and John had an epic knock-down, drag-out everyone here heard."

Milly fished. "About Sabrina Navas."

"Who else? I mean, Navas *has* been acting—" She shot her a glance. "Look, I don't want to get in trouble. Could you hand me that container?"

Milly passed her a large tray. The keeper dropped the chunks of meat in with wet plops. The bullet-damaged piece landed on top. Milly stared at it as the evidence she'd gathered coalesced.

The thermal image Luther had shown the detective. It hadn't looked right. There'd been no hot red halo of a fresh puncture. And when Maskwa had attacked from her cell, she'd moved as if there'd been no muscle damage from being shot.

Luther Nikolai had lied about Maskwa's injury. There was no bullet wound. Which meant Carin had missed the bear with all five shots.

But Milly had counted four bullet holes in the surgical suite, including the one through the security door, where Doyle Amon had said he'd stood during the attack. That evidence made no sense, unless …

Unless the gun Carin had used as her last line of defense was defective. Unless the damage to the surgical suite had been staged.

* * *

MILLY STEPPED out of the Zoo-ber—the BioPark's zero-emission ridesharing service—at the end of the residential street. Any one of the people she'd questioned today could be a murderer. But Milly's meetings with Dr. Appleton and Doyle Amon had been in public spaces. Even with Luther Nikolai, there'd been witnesses who'd seen them together as they'd walked to Maskwa's cell. While she didn't believe John Radebe had harmed Carin or would hurt Milly herself, she wasn't stupid enough to take that chance. The ridesharing driver would be her witness. She asked him to pick her up at John's one-bedroom bungalow in forty-five minutes.

Hands in her jacket pockets, she hurried down the tidy street. She'd been offered a home in Cambrian Village on admittance to her PhD program, which was odd since they were usually kept as loyalty rewards or given to support staff with families. But she was happy with her condo complex discreetly embedded near the heart of the zoo. She loved sitting out on her balcony in the morning and sipping coffee, listening to the waking de-extincts—the trumpeting rumbles of the *Cuvieronius* herd, the rolling coos of dodos, the dire wolves' singing barks.

Set in the rise and fall of land at the edge of the Rio Grande Forest, Cambrian Village consisted of over three hundred minimal-impact energy-efficient homes built specifically for the Pleistocene BioPark. Everything a person needed was in meticulously planned micro neighborhoods—diverse restaurants; bookstore cafés and coffee shops; organic groceries and sundries stores; sports parks, gyms, and pools; walking trails; health-provider clinics; salons and barbers; saloons and bars; and small but colorful casinos. School-aged children attended well-equipped learning hubs. Community centers, houses of worship, and day cares were within walking distance from every home. Anything else needed or wanted could be ordered online.

Engineered animals and engineered lifestyles.

John's front door opened wide as Milly approached, John yanking on a T-shirt. He looked tired, his expression pulled and dispirited, eyes red rimmed.

She smiled at him. "Remind me to kill the cameras tonight."

"You *are* planning to finish Maskwa's surgery without permission. Luther stopped by earlier and warned me what you could be up to." He stepped to one side as he ushered her into his home.

Milly wrinkled her nose. "I might have given myself away when he took me to Maskwa after our meeting with the police. I became quite … animated."

He smiled, white teeth in dark skin. "That's not like you, Milly. Normally so calm and controlled. He was shaken by it."

"I've never seen Luther Nikolai truly shaken about anything." She stopped at the long counter that divided a sleek kitchen from the great room. "Will you tell him?"

John stood barefoot in slouchy black basketball shorts. With his arms crossed, the T-shirt stretched over the smooth bunched muscles of his wide shoulders and chest.

"I've already sworn not to help." But his smile made the statement a lie.

Relief blanketed her. Only one more person to ask.

"I can supply prepared flash sticks and the sedation gun and get us into Maskwa's holding cell," he continued, "but I don't have access to the surgical equipment or other medications."

"There's always Appleton's hidden access fob, but I have a well-stocked emergency kit." She gave him an impish smile. "You'd be surprised what can be slipped away and not found even with the most stringent audit."

He laughed deeply. "'She is like a diamond with hidden facets.' Not my words, Milly Smith. What else is underneath that proper exterior we don't know about?" And he looked at her with more interest than he'd ever done in the past.

Milly's cheeks heated. Whose words, then? Luther's? She shied away from her thoughts and said, "Tell me what happened. I don't remember."

That sobered him immediately. "You haven't watched the video?"

"No, but I've questioned Appleton and his tech, Doyle Amon. I asked Amon to assist tonight. He's on board."

"Amon is ... interesting. He was brought in unexpectedly a few weeks ago to replace someone who didn't need replacing. Coffee?" She shook her head, and John poured himself a cup. "He watches too closely. I don't know that I like him."

"Would he have had a reason to cause Carin harm?"

His shoulders stiffened. "You mean like me?"

He didn't roll out the official BioPark statement about Carin's death being a terrible accident.

"And others. Sabrina. Luther. About the only thing I remember from the surgery was that Luther was there, in the observation area. When I asked, he told me Carin wanted to speak to him after Maskwa's surgery. I assume it must have been important, because he came." She paused, tilting her head. "Do you know what it was about?"

John sipped his coffee and shrugged. "Whatever it was is moot now, isn't it?" He pinned his gaze on her. "Besides, Luther would never want you or Carin harmed. You know, he tried to open the door to the surgical suite—against protocol—to let you out."

Milly stared at John, jolted by his words. That's not what Amon had said.

"Luther was more than shocked to see you there instead of Appleton. That whole rushed transition was messed up, and Appleton knows it. He's been trying to cover his ass ever since."

"I know Amon was told not to talk about the rushed transition to the police."

He shrugged again. "It was thought to be for the best."

"Everyone was told to lie about it?"

"More a sin of omission. Let's just say the police never asked that question."

"There wasn't just one sin of omission. Tell me about the gun, John."

He blinked at her, mouth slightly open. Seconds ticked by. She maintained his shocked stare, hiding growing excitement. She'd been right. Something was up with the gun.

John started to laugh.

"My God, Milly. We underestimate you at our own peril."

She wondered if by *we* he meant himself and Luther.

"How did you figure that out?" he asked.

"Little details that added up. Amon said he watched Carin shoot Maskwa and was surprised when I told him she'd missed the bear four out of five times. He told me that he saw Luther load the backup sedative on your flash stick and inject Maskwa through the bars. He saw Maskwa lay down and put her head in my lap instead of killing me. The only place he could have seen all those events is through the security door's window." She paused. "Except there's a bullet hole through that door, right where he said he was standing. Why isn't he dead?"

Milly waited, but John said nothing.

"The one bullet that allegedly hit Maskwa remains lodged in a fat pad," she continued. "Luther showed a heat profile of that area to the police in the meeting this morning, except it didn't look right. And when we visited Maskwa earlier today, she almost killed me through the cage bars using the foreleg from the supposedly damaged side of her body. I guess it's possible that her wound is superficial, but I keep wondering how a bullet strong enough to punch through a steel security door didn't blow apart Maskwa's chest and shoulder."

"Because after Maskwa was sedated for her checkup, you found a mammary gland infection along with her bad tooth. The heat profile Luther showed the police was one that you'd saved."

Milly nodded slowly. That could explain Luther's reluctance to help her. "What happened once I found the mammary infection?"

"You administered the antibiotic, and the bear revived shortly afterward." He stopped again, swallowing deeply. "Then everything went to hell."

She pushed. "John? What's going on?"

He pulled in a long breath. "The bear's not dead, but Carin Zuanick is because the gun was an e-gun, all sound and fury, signifying nothing."

Milly's knees seemed to melt. She braced her hands against the counter. It was the same conclusion she'd come to, but to have it confirmed....

"Who switched the guns?" Changing out the gun pointed to premeditation.

John carefully placed his coffee cup on the countertop and spread his hands flat on either side of it. He leveled his gaze at her. "Do you think it was me?"

Truth be told, she didn't know. She wasn't even sure John had motive to be rid of Carin, except maybe anger at the way she'd treated Sabrina. People had murdered for less.

The CCTV camera was manual, turned on and off to record the surgery, so both John and Sabrina had opportunity to switch guns before it had been turned on. Luther could've done it earlier, too, as could have Appleton or Amon.

But in all the years Milly had been involved with surgeries on de-extincts, never had the gun been used to stop an animal. It was pure bad luck the surgery had gone so wrong that the weapon would be necessary.

Unless more than just the gun switch had occurred.

Unless Maskwa had been meant to wake up.

"During police questioning this morning, they said I called for you to administer more sedation, and you initially deployed the green stick. The green stick has the revival medicine." Milly stared at him. He averted his gaze. Her mouth dried. "Except it didn't this time, did it?"

John lifted panicked eyes. He pivoted away from her, but she scurried around to stay in his sight.

"You switched the drugs, didn't you? The green stick had the sedation syringe," she said. "That's why you deployed it first. You couldn't go through with your plan because I was caught inside the suite with

Carin. You didn't realize I'd been switched to lead. That I was supposed to be the last one out of the room."

The raw pain on John's face triggered a horrible flash of remembrance. Of screaming, pleading. Of Sabrina tugging at his arm.

"But when I called you out, you switched back to the red stick and injected what you *knew* to be the revival drug. Carin or I would be forced to use the gun to kill Maskwa, except the gun was fake. You doomed us, John. You doomed Maskwa."

His eyes squeezed shut. The hard creases filled with tears.

"I didn't replace the gun, I swear. I *never* meant to hurt you or Carin," he said, voice thick. "I wasn't the one who switched out the drugs."

"John, *no*," a woman's voice cried.

Milly whirled to find Sabrina Navas standing across the living area, barefoot in a tank and shorts, her hair wrapped up in a towel.

"I couldn't let Sabrina get caught." His eyes pleaded.

"John, you *promised*," Sabrina wailed.

He swallowed. "Milly, she's pregnant. It's my baby."

CHAPTER NINE

SABRINA SAT HUNCHED ON THE SOFA, HER DEEP AUBURN hair in damp ropes down her back, John next to her, all four of their hands tangled together. On edge, Milly settled in a chair across from them, hiding clenched hands behind folded arms.

"I was just so angry," Sabrina said bitterly, her Spanish accent thick. "When I thought John wasn't looking, I switched the two vials on his flash sticks. It was stupid and impulsive...." She tugged away one hand and reached out in supplication to Milly. "I never thought—I mean, it's so rare that John has to deploy more sedative; it shouldn't have made a difference, you know? It was just another small stab of defiance against Carin and—and her *sabotage* of me."

"I think you hated her, too," Milly said.

It was like a switch was flipped.

"God, that *witch*," Sabrina hissed.

Milly exchanged a wide-eyed glance with John. His return look mirrored hers.

"She was jealous of me. She knew—*knew*—I was a better vet than she was. She pretended to support me. Pretended to help me pass the licensing test to practice here. But she really made sure I would fail, over and over. It was her fault, not mine."

She broke away from John's touch and stood, movements jerky and agitated.

"You know, she would say it would be good to have two de-extinct dentists because the work was so demanding, but she didn't really mean it. She wanted all the glory, all the power. None for me." Sabrina paced to an open area in the room. "I am going to take that test again and then take her position here in the BioPark."

Milly's lips thinned. *Is that why she switched out the vials? Because she thought with Carin gone, she could completely replace her?* Like she'd replaced Carin in John's bed.

"The things I did were foolish," Sabrina continued hotly. "But she had no right to fire me."

Things. Plural.

"Sabrina?" Milly asked. "Were the instruments you handed Carin during the surgery the ones she asked for?"

The young woman seemed to deflate. "No. None of them."

"*Sabrina.*" John went to her. He grasped her shoulders and turned her gently. "Why?"

She flared again. "Because she'd slept with you, too. Because she said you and I would never last. Because she said I was unstable and unfit to work with de-extincts." Her whole body quivered with tension, mouth an ugly curl, her brown eyes like hot coals. Then the fire within her extinguished. "I'm tired, John. I want to go lie down." She cradled one hand against her stomach and looked at Milly. "Can I go?"

"One more question. Did you touch the gun? The one Carin used?"

Her brows knit. "No. Only the vials."

That was bad enough. Milly had wanted Sabrina as part of Maskwa's surgery that evening, but the woman was exhibiting too many hard emotions that seemed beyond her control.

John wrapped an arm around Sabrina's shoulders and walked her to the bedroom door. She pulled away from him to face Milly once more.

"Carin's death was actually your fault, you know. You always bring another syringe of sedative, but you didn't use it. Instead, you asked John to intervene. That means you won't tell, right? Because you could get into trouble, too. No one else knows what I did, what *we* did, but us here in this room. It would mean the end of our careers. We could even get arrested." She lifted her face to John's and plucked at his T-shirt. "She won't tell, will she? Make sure she doesn't tell, John."

"I'll talk to Dr. Smith about it, *mon ange*. You go rest." He kissed her forehead and closed the door behind her.

"I didn't use my syringe of sedative?" Milly asked him. She always brought more propofol, enough for two extra minutes' sedation to get everyone out of the surgical suite. She would drop the syringe in her lab coat pocket so it was on her person in case she was away from the instrument carts.

"Maybe you didn't draw because of the rushed transition." John paused. "Milly? With the stress of her pregnancy, Sabrina hasn't been herself lately. She's, ah, taken herself off certain prescription medications because she's afraid they will hurt the baby. It has made her more ... erratic."

Milly made a quick connection.

"The fight you and Carin had at the bear grotto. What was it about?"

He rubbed a hand over his face. "Sabrina's behavior. I thought Carin was just there to malign Sabrina because she was jealous, so I got angry. I didn't listen. Maybe I didn't want to know."

"Other people have noticed, John. In fact, that's why Carin asked Luther to attend the surgery, isn't it? Because she wanted him to see firsthand what Sabrina might be capable of. Because she was going to tell him afterwards about her ... instability."

John dropped his gaze, his lack of response confirming Milly's supposition.

"What Sabrina did directly contributed to Carin's death. She might not have meant anything, but it won't be long before admin starts to ask more questions."

A hard laugh burst from him. "There you are wrong, Dr. Smith.

Only you and Luther have delved deeper. The BioPark board wants this incident wrapped up and thrown out with yesterday's garbage. The surgery you're planning might relieve Maskwa's immediate pain, but it's futile. They'll choose to euthanize her in the end because they won't have the famous killer bear on exhibition. Maskwa would only give groups that oppose de-extinction a platform to protest on."

"I don't care," Milly said fiercely. "What happened to her was cruel. Something she didn't deserve. I'll continue to fight for her."

"The BioPark is worth a king's ransom. The board would do anything to protect that wealth. I believe they threatened Luther and Kingbird, even Appleton's job. Your fight might lose you *yours*."

Milly lifted her chin. "Why am I any more important than Maskwa? Because I'm human and she's just an animal? Maybe it's time we change our thinking about the value of life. Are you still willing to help me tonight?"

"Yes. I owe it to Carin. And Maskwa." His eyes shadowed. "Will you tell Luther what Sabrina and I did?"

Now it was Milly's turn to hesitate. "She needs to get some help."

"She has an appointment with a doctor in Santa Fe next week. She wants no one at the BioPark to know about her pregnancy yet."

She hedged. "I'll have to think about it."

"You didn't ask Sabrina to participate in Maskwa's surgery." It was almost a question.

"I'll finish the procedure myself, although I might need to pull Maskwa's tooth instead of trying to save it."

"I can come in the cage and help."

"No. Amon will be inside the enclosure with me. If I need help, I'll ask him. You'll be outside the cage with your flash sticks. By the book." It had been forty-five minutes. Milly headed to the front door. Hand on the knob, she paused. "John? Did Sabrina have anything to do with the gun switch?"

"No. And neither did I. I don't even want her to know about it; that would only upset her more. She's barely stopped crying since Carin's death. Yes, Sabrina's actions were rash, done out of emotion.

But the gun switch was obviously planned, which means someone else had a hand in Carin's death."

John might believe Sabrina, but Milly wasn't so sure. Sabrina's hatred of Carin Zuanick had obviously been building over time. Elements preceding Carin's death appeared so random and disordered, they pointed to someone irrational. And John had been a willing participant in covering for the future mother of his child.

But if what he'd said was true and neither of them had replaced the gun, then there was someone else still out there.

A horn honked outside. Her driver was here. "Who shot up the surgical suite?" she asked.

"Luther, after we cleared the room. He took a live fire pistol from the BioPark's range collection. That's the one the police confiscated for evidence."

"What about the weapon the e-gun replaced?"

John's face pulled into a frown. "That gun is still missing."

CHAPTER TEN

MILLY UNLOCKED HER CONDO DOOR AND STEPPED INSIDE, absorbing the peace that came with being home. Each step dragged after she'd left John's house. Her shoulder throbbed, and a headache was poised just behind her eyes. Even though she'd successfully assembled her surgical team, she still had details to finalize. But she remained very aware that every hour, every minute that passed meant Maskwa was suffering.

She couldn't—*wouldn't*—let Maskwa down.

Pulling out her phone, she sent Luther a text.

I want to watch the CCTV of Maskwa's surgery.

Her message was read immediately. Dots pulsed on the screen.

Difficult to watch. Would you like company? I can be at your place in 20 min.

Milly sat down, stomach flipping. He knew where she lived?

Idiot. He could easily look it up on the staff database.

She tapped in, *I'd rather watch it alone.*

Nothing for lingering seconds. Milly nibbled the corner of her lip. Was he upset at her reply?

First code provides access to Channel 1003—an in-park secure channel

—second code to access the video. Once the video is started, there's a three-hour window before access is lost.

Terse. Impersonal.

Thank you

He didn't reply.

* * *

Milly ate a late lunch and worked out drug specifications as she outlined the protocol for that evening's surgery. She attached her finished product and messaged it to John and Amon, requesting that they prepare the sedation and antidotes. An hour before sunset, she set her alarm and laid down to rest, but her mind raced, and when she finally drifted to sleep, it was littered with dreams and nightmares. When she woke, her shoulder at least felt better, and the slight headache that had stalked her all day was gone.

She didn't start the CCTV video until nine o'clock, watched carefully as Carin requested instruments and Sabrina handed her the wrong ones on purpose. Once fired, Sabrina dashed away, brushing up against Milly as she exited the suite. But the camera coverage was limited. Milly couldn't follow her movements after she was out the security door, except …

Sabrina's face did appear briefly in the window, cheeks slick with tears, mouth twisted in anguish. Milly froze the picture, shivering at the hatred in her eyes. Sabrina might have purposely pricked Carin's temper, but she'd been shocked when Carin had actually fired her. The video validated Sabrina's account of impulsively switching the flash-stick vials out of anger.

Then John deliberately used the wrong flash stick.

He'd said that he'd been protecting Sabrina from her rash actions. His own actions during the surgery had been stupid, but people committed stupid—and courageous—acts to protect the ones they loved.

John Radebe didn't want Carin dead or Milly hurt. She believed him.

Milly restarted the recording. Sound wasn't great on the raw video, and she had to strain to hear Carin's threat to expose Luther's secrets. She watched as Doyle Amon placed the antibiotics in her hand, anticipating her request. She watched as she injected the drug into the line in Maskwa's front leg. Within seconds, the bear's paw twitched.

John was right. Maskwa began to revive immediately after she'd pushed in the antibiotic. Milly rewound and zoomed in to study the syringe, but nothing looked off, the antibiotic the same volume that Appleton had written in his calculations. Besides, antibiotic alone wouldn't revive the bear.

Unless it was mixed with antidote.

Appleton was known for letting his techs do most of his prep work. Had the rhino emergency been a false alarm to get Appleton away from the surgery? One that would let Amon tamper with Maskwa's drugs? Gavin Appleton might have had an indirect hand in Carin's death because of the rushed handoff to Milly, but nothing more. Milly eliminated him.

Besides, he didn't have a motive to kill Carin. At least, not one as overt as Sabrina's.

Sabrina would've prepped for Carin and had access to the medications. Had she tainted the antibiotic? But if her shocked expression was any indication, she hadn't expected to be fired. And if she hadn't been fired, she would've been present when Maskwa revived so wouldn't have had the opportunity to switch flash-stick vials. Sabrina's acts were impulsive, not premeditated—well, except the incorrect instruments. With reluctance, Milly took her off her list of suspects.

That left Doyle Amon and Luther Nikolai.

Milly hit play and continued to watch.

Appleton's testimony at the morning briefing matched the visual of Amon's retreat after she instigated revival protocol, except it wasn't orderly. The Milly on-screen had been knocked back by a full-body collision as the tech withdrew.

As Amon exited, CCTV Milly slid her hand in her scrubs pocket and retrieved nothing. *No extra syringe of sedative.* She searched the instrument trays, the floor, gloved hands scrabbling. She called for John to intervene.

Milly rewound again and focused on Amon. He slapped the thinscreen to open the security door, his second hand in his scrubs pocket. When the door closed behind him, his face appeared in the window alongside Luther's.

Luther. He'd told Milly that Carin had invited him to the surgery so they could talk afterward, but he hadn't explained why. Because it was personal, between him and his ex?

Or because it was a *personnel* issue about Sabrina Navas and her ability to work with dangerous de-extincts, something John had all but confirmed when Milly had confronted him at his home. That meant Carin's big talk about spilling Luther's secrets was an empty threat, a display of her power to Sabrina and John.

Luther had also been the one person who'd saved Milly by injecting Maskwa with more sedative.

But Doyle Amon had accused Luther of refusing to open the security door.

Milly pressed play and zoomed in to watch Carin futilely slap on the thinscreen controls, then pound on the heavy metal door. Amon's and Luther's faces disappeared from the window, but Milly couldn't tell what was going on outside the operating room, so she couldn't confirm Amon's statement that Luther had blocked the door, or John's that Luther had tried to open it and let them escape.

She paused the video and sat back. Dr. Luther Nikolai was methodical and focused—and ruthless. If he'd wanted Carin dead, his plans wouldn't have been this laughable mixture of premeditation and bad luck.

She dismissed Luther from her suspect list.

The rest was difficult to watch. Carin pounding and pleading at the door. Milly, an arm's length behind her, spinning and looking up. Maskwa's enormous paw swinging. She watched herself fly across the room, heard the thud of her body against the wall, observed herself sliding to a collapse, head listing, arms slack. Carin ducked past the raging bear, grabbed the gun. She took her last stand across from the security door. The window displayed only Amon's face now. Luther was gone.

The gunshots were deafening. By the third report Carin's face contorted with absolute terror. Tears started in Milly's eyes as Carin continued shooting, but Carin knew. The gun was worthless, the sound signifying her horrific death.

Milly turned away at Carin's screams. When they ended, they were replaced by men's shouts and the keening of Sabrina Navas. Milly wiped her eyes and turned back to watch the final minutes of the video. Luther's shirt-sleeved arm thrust through the bars; a flash stick jabbed at Maskwa. The bear swiped, knocking the stick away. She dropped to all fours and charged the bars, slammed into them. Then her huge body sagged, the sedative taking effect. She fought it, punching a foreleg tipped with blood-darkened claws between metal bars. But this time, the sedative won.

The camera looked down from above as the woozy bear retreated. Maskwa staggered to where Milly slumped against the wall, lay down, and, with a bellowed sigh, put her head in Milly's lap. Milly's hand lifted to stroke Maskwa's head, like she had when the bear was a tiny cub and needed reassurance. A soft humming now competed with Sabrina's quiet sobs, and Milly recognized a lullaby her mother sang to her as a small child.

Doyle Amon's face stayed framed in the security door's window the whole time. He hadn't moved, hadn't flinched, even when the gun had been pointed and discharged in his direction. If Amon had once been a Russian soldier, he'd know how dangerous being in the line of fire was.

Unless he knew the gun was useless.

Milly grabbed the controller and quickly rewound to Amon's exit from the room. She slowed the tape and zoomed in, watched him bump her hard, then thrust his hand in his pocket.

Milly paused the video, breathing unsteadily. *Had he pocketed my backup syringe of sedative?* It was the only thing that made sense.

She ran through her evidence against Doyle Amon again. He could've sent the anonymous emergency summons to Appleton, then tampered with the surgical drugs. He could've lied about Luther and the door. With his access to the surgical suite, he could've easily switched out the gun.

It all fit together in a neat package. Had Milly invited Carin's murderer to that night's surgery?

Except ...

Milly had been called in to Maskwa's surgery that day to replace Appleton. *She'd* been switched to lead, something Appleton denied doing. He thought she'd made the change, but Milly knew she was too by the book, too *boring* to take that step, which meant someone else at the surgery had changed her to lead.

The hair prickled on her neck.

Milly rewound, this time focusing on Carin. The woman stood as if turned to salt, staring into the bear's face, some primitive foci of her brain triggering frozen panic. Dr. Appleton experienced a similar kind of involuntary response, although with a different physiological outcome.

But how someone responded under that kind of pressure was unpredictable. If Carin hadn't frozen the way she had, she would've been out the door, right behind Amon. As lead, the only one left in the room would have been Milly. That was predictable.

The last person in the room with Maskwa. Her head spun dizzily.

That meant *she* had been Doyle Amon's target. And she'd just handed him a second chance.

A second chance. He'd said it himself at the café. At the time, she'd thought he'd been talking about helping Maskwa, but what if he'd meant a second opportunity to kill Milly?

She stood. Hands laced over her head, she paced. She'd call Luther or Kingbird or Detective Roman, tell them her conclusions, let the authorities take over. She stopped in her tracks. Then what would happen to Maskwa? The bear wouldn't get relief from her suffering, and nothing about this mess was Maskwa's fault.

Milly would go forward with the surgery—with precautions.

Calm settled over her as she sorted through details. She'd asked Amon and John to draw the medications, a mistake she'd remedy by bringing the drugs from her emergency stock. Her blood pounding, she texted her conspirators with a time and asked for any questions, telling them this would be the equivalent of a presurgical meeting. They texted back they were ready.

Based on her analysis of the botched surgery and her reassessment of the evidence, very little else needed to change in her plans that evening. If all went to plan, she'd not only relieve Maskwa of her pain but catch a murderer at the same time.

Then she would leverage her success to save Maskwa's life. Because her bear had been used as a murder weapon, and that really ticked her off.

There were still a few details she needed to take care of. First, she reset the video at half speed. If anyone was monitoring her, they'd think she was still watching the tape when she'd actually be leading Maskwa's surgery. Next, she tapped in another text. She'd wait until she stepped into the bear's cage to hit send. She hadn't questioned John without a witness to her whereabouts, and she wouldn't go into this surgery without one, either. Finally, she opened her personal gun safe and, without hesitation, pulled a pistol that took bullets large enough to stop a bear. She checked it.

Predictable, careful, boring Milly Smith. Everything planned down to the final detail.

By the book.

Milly slipped the gun into her medical satchel and closed the safe. Throwing a trench coat over her scrubs, she left the condo and headed underground. This time, she used a hover pod.

When she arrived at Maskwa's cell, Doyle Amon and John Radebe were waiting for her.

So was Sabrina Navas.

CHAPTER ELEVEN

THE ROOM CONTAINING MASKWA'S CELL WAS WARM, AND sweat filmed Milly's skin. But the stench of the bear and waste was much less pungent. Milly quickly assessed Maskwa. On all fours, no rocking, focused and alert with the number of people present. The bear watched them all warily, her jaw swollen, her mouth open and drooling. But she'd been washed, as had the floor of her confinement pen. That accounted for the warm air. Whoever had ordered the cleaning—probably John—had wanted the bear comfortable and dry.

"Excuse me for being late. I wanted to make sure the camera was off. Everyone, keep back from the bars until Maskwa is sedated. She has a pretty good reach between them. John?" Milly nodded to Sabrina. The woman's presence set Milly's teeth on edge, a complication she hadn't factored into her master plan.

"I'm sorry, Milly. She insisted on coming," John said.

"Don't speak like I'm not here." Sabrina pushed forward, mouth mulish. She stood a couple of inches taller than Milly, so she looked down her nose. "You don't think I can help, do you? You're just like Carin."

Milly propped her hands on her hips. "I'm not, but Carin was right. You're not fit to work with de-extincts right now. You need to leave."

"Then I go straight to security, and Maskwa won't get help."

Milly shifted mentally. Big picture, it didn't matter who dealt with Maskwa's tooth, so long as it got done. "Fine, you can stay. But no root canal. Maskwa's too weak for a long sedation. Pull her tooth and treat the wound. That's all."

Sabrina smiled triumphantly.

Milly stripped off her coat. She looked around the room for a place to hang it and chose the old lever that once raised and lowered the panel to the back area. That entry to the bear's sleeping area was closed now to keep Maskwa in the front portion of her cell. A cart stood near the closed cage entrance, gleaming metal tray on top.

"As requested, I've prepped a tray, Dr. Smith," Amon said. His light blue scrubs hung loose on his lean body. He'd already gloved.

"Appleton's secret-access fob?" she asked with a smile.

He nodded, lips quirking before adjusting his mask over his mouth and nose. "It allowed me to gather everything I needed."

Milly perused the tray, ticking off the items: a syringe filled with antibiotics, a second labeled with the sedation medication, the razor to shave Maskwa's foreleg, and instruments necessary for a venous line as well as for a root canal or tooth extraction.

"I won't need your draws. I decided to prepare all the medications myself to avoid … mistakes."

Amon frowned. "But you asked—"

Milly swept up the filled syringes and dropped them into a drawer built into the cart.

"Same with yours, John. And thank you for cleaning up Maskwa."

"I cannot take credit for that." He met her surprised gaze as he handed her the sedation dart before carefully detaching the syringes that tipped his flash sticks. She placed them in the top drawer of the cart and locked it.

Milly dug in her bag and handed John a sedative-filled dart along with the prepared syringes for his flash sticks and watched carefully as he prepped, double-checking that the medications were correctly loaded. She placed her draws on the tray—antibiotic, extra sedative, and, for Sabrina, a large plastic bottle of sterile saline and an empty fifty-milliliter wash syringe.

"John, you will stay outside the cage. Don't come in for any reason. I've set up sedation for approximately fifteen minutes. By my calculations, Dr. Navas, Mr. Amon, and I should only be in the cage with Maskwa for ten. Oh, and..."

With deliberate care, she pulled out the handgun and laid it at the top of the instrument tray. She met everyone's eyes.

"This is a dangerous de-extinct, so by the book, people. Let's do this fast and get out of here. Better on the bear, better on us. John?"

He nodded and darted Maskwa.

The bear jerked, opening her mouth and releasing a low-pitched moan of confusion and fright. Milly's heart squeezed. Maskwa fought the sedation, but within less than three minutes, she crumpled to the cement floor. Milly grimaced at the bear's position on the side of the cell, opposite to the cage door and far from the thinscreen control. If Maskwa revived unexpectedly, it would take longer for them to retreat from the danger.

"Not the best placement," John said, echoing Milly's thoughts. Through the bars, he prodded Maskwa with the butt end of his red flash stick. Nothing. "Ready?" He strode to the thinscreen, tapped it, and the cage door swung open. He then tapped his wrist tech. "Fifteen minutes."

Amon rolled in the cart, instruments and gun rattling on the metal tray, followed by Sabrina.

"How will you get to her bullet wound?" Sabrina asked.

"That's already been taken care of," Milly replied.

Sabrina's eyes held confusion. "When?"

John had sworn Sabrina didn't know the guns had been switched, which would mean she'd still believe that Maskwa had been wounded. Sabrina's confusion was a point in her favor.

"The antibiotics I drew will suppress any infection." Milly glanced at Doyle Amon, who appeared to be listening intently. "That wound doesn't seem to bother Maskwa that much anyway."

"Just worry about the tooth, *ma chérie*," John said. "I want this over and you safe."

Milly paused at the threshold. If what she believed was true, Doyle Amon was a murderer, and she was not only putting herself in danger but the others as well.

Did she have that right?

Her gaze dropped to the sedated bear, and she stiffened her spine. Maskwa was what mattered. It was her duty to save this creature she'd helped create. She pulled out her phone and sent the text she'd composed at her condo. Now Luther knew she'd gone against his direct order, but he was also her witness if something untoward happened. It vibrated back almost immediately, but she ignored the reply and pocketed the phone.

She stepped into the cage. John tapped the screen again. The cage door clanged shut with a fading vibration of sound. He hurried back to stand outside the bars within flash-stick distance of the sedated bear.

Maskwa lay sprawled on her stomach, jaw held to the cement floor by her boulder-sized head. Milly knelt by the bear and pressed her hands into the damp fur. Maskwa's heart thumped slowly under her palms.

"Front right leg," Milly directed Amon. He powered up the razor to shave an area above the bear's paw so Milly could insert her venous line for the antibiotics.

"Her head isn't in a great position for me to get to the tooth," Sabrina said, extraction forceps in hand. She'd sidled into place on the left side of the sleeping bear, sandwiched between Maskwa's bulk and the cage bars. "I'll need help."

Milly nodded to Amon. He edged between Maskwa's paws, squatted, and slid his gloved hands into Maskwa's mouth, his back against the cage bars. He had a little more room than Sabrina, but not much.

"Four minutes gone," John announced.

"Now," Sabrina said, and Amon lifted, grunting with the weight of the bear's head and neck. She pried open the jaw.

Milly kept an eye on their work but continued threading the line into Maskwa's leg. She had plenty of room to maneuver, the bulk of the open cage behind her.

"More," Sabrina ordered. "I can't get to…"

Amon grunted again as he thrust upward, scrubs pulled tight over bulging thighs and rounded shoulders, arms corded with strain. Sabrina grabbed the rotten tooth with the extractors and pulled. It popped out, followed by the stench of infection. She tossed the instrument and an enormous canine onto the cement with a clatter.

"Seven minutes gone," John droned.

"Keep her mouth open while I clean the—keep her mouth open!" Sabrina cried.

"I'm sorry. It's … heavy." Amon turned his face, red with strain, to John. "Mr. Radebe? Can you come in for a moment to help?"

Milly's skin prickled.

"Milly?" John asked. He stood poised on the walkway outside the cage, near the bear's rear flank.

"No." She flushed the line in Maskwa's wrist and locked on the syringe of antibiotic. She held Doyle Amon's gaze. He was close enough for her to pick out the blue-gray ring around his brown irises. "John would need to put down his flash stick and leave the cage door open while he was inside. That would make it easier for you, wouldn't it?" she asked quietly.

Amon tensed.

"Perfect. Just like that." Sabrina flushed the ragged red hole in Maskwa's mouth with saline. "I might have to throw in a stitch or two. Let me get them." She stood and edged around the bear, hurrying to the instrument cart.

Milly continued to push the powerful antibiotic into Maskwa's vein. "You have a syringe of antidote in your pocket." She glanced at the tight fabric at Amon's crotch that stretched over a long cylindrical bulge. "Or are you just happy to see me? Once John was inside the cage, were you going to deploy it and lock us in? Use Maskwa as your murder weapon like you did with Carin?"

"This man murdered Carin?" John's voice shook.

"Yes. But she was collateral damage, like you and Sabrina were meant to be tonight. I'm his target."

"Why?" John asked.

"I don't know. When Luther arrives, we'll get to the bottom of it," Milly said, and Amon's eyes widened above his mask. "Time?"

"Nine minutes gone. You called Luther?"

"I texted him to come here before I walked into the cage."

"I was to contact him after the surgery was over." John slid ice-cold eyes over Doyle Amon. "I didn't keep Carin or you safe last time, but now … if this man makes the slightest move, he dies."

Amon's eyes rolled in John's direction. The red flash stick with its needle was poised within an inch of Amon's throat.

Milly removed the line from Maskwa and taped the wound. She stood.

"Get up," she ordered Amon. "Hands on your head."

"But I'm not done yet." Sabrina fiddled with the instrument tray behind her.

Amon released the bear and stood, raising his hands, the flash stick now close enough to prick his skin.

Milly reached into his pocket and pulled out a filled syringe. She stepped back.

"I couldn't figure out why you didn't mention the bullet hole in the security door when we talked. It could've killed you. *Should've* killed you. After I watched the CCTV video, I realized you knew nothing about the shot through the door. How could that be? The only thing I could come up with was that the damage to the surgical suite was staged. John confirmed that when he told me Luther shot up the room afterward as part of a cover-up. That meant the gun Carin used was an e-weapon. It looked and sounded like the real thing but wasn't." Milly shook her head, her gaze never leaving his. "You mixed the antibiotic with antidote, knowing it could be blamed on Dr. Appleton and his failing memory. You switched out the gun, knowing it could be blamed on John, who was distracted by a very public feud between Carin and Sabrina. When I triggered the revival protocol, you bumped me as you left and took my backup syringe of sedative. Then you stood at the door to watch your handiwork play out, knowing you weren't in any danger."

"You believe he's the one responsible for Carin's death?" Sabrina asked. She'd turned to face them.

"Yes, but so are you and John," Milly said. "And me. We all are because we didn't proceed by the book."

Tears started in Sabrina's eyes. She yanked off her mask. "This is a setup? We're going to lose our jobs and go to jail."

"My goal has always been to save Maskwa, but everything will have to come out now." Milly leveled her gaze at Sabrina. "I don't think you'll go to jail, but if it means the loss of my job and yours, so be it."

"Just like Carin." Sabrina let out a sob. She raised her arm. The deadly eye of the gun was aimed directly at Milly's forehead. "But this is *my* life. And you don't get to make that decision."

Milly's mind reeled. She'd been *wrong*? But every detail, every clue pointed to Amon. Except …

Sabrina's plaintive voice echoed in her head: *Make sure she doesn't tell.*

"Sabrina, *no!*" John jerked, and the end of the flash stick shifted away from Amon's neck. Amon leaped over the bear and out of reach. Sabrina swung the muzzle toward him and backed to the cage door.

"John, don't you understand?" she said, eyes alight, an odd smile stretching her lips. "The camera's off. We can say Maskwa revived and I had to use the gun and accidently killed them both. If Carin missed so many times, why can't I?"

"Because it was all a lie, sweetheart. The gun Carin used wasn't real. Fifteen minutes gone, Milly."

Sabrina pressed against the closed cage door. "Looks like time's up."

Calm settled over Milly.

And Sabrina pulled the trigger.

CHAPTER TWELVE

THE BOOM OF THE SHOT ECHOED OFF THE CEMENT WALLS, ringing in Milly's ears. A second shot followed, and a third.

Sabrina's face twisted into a rictus of astonishment. "You said by the book. *By the book.*" She aimed and shot again.

"I lied," Milly replied simply. "About the camera, too. I turned it on."

The chamber door to the outside hall slammed against the wall. Luther Nikolai burst into the room. Maskwa heaved a deep breath. Her paw twitched.

"She's reviving," Milly called. "Open the door."

Luther slapped the thinscreen, and the cage door unlatched. Amon rushed Sabrina. He grabbed her around the waist and placed a scalpel against her neck. She dropped Milly's e-gun.

"Don't follow or I'll puncture her carotid," he said, using Sabrina as his shield against the nasty black gun that appeared in Luther's hands. His eyes crinkled, like he was smiling behind his mask. "You figured out quite a lot. I honestly didn't think it would work." His gaze pierced Milly. "Technically, it didn't."

He pulled the whimpering Sabrina out of the cage and slammed the barred door, leaving Milly inside with Maskwa. He shouldered open the keeper's access to the bear's sleeping area, and he and Sabrina slipped through. From inside that room, he had access to the BioPark's extensive underground passages and could easily disappear.

Maskwa lifted a wobbly head, eyes blinking. Milly skirted the bars toward the cage door. The bear caught her movement, her head turning to follow. She huffed, and Milly's stomach knotted.

"The door. *Open the door.*" She clutched the bars, heart beating so hard it was ready to explode.

The thinscreen blinked out under Luther's hand. Maskwa stood and, swaying, rotated toward Milly.

"Disabled," John said. "Amon must have—" He grabbed the red flash stick and jammed the sedative into Maskwa's side.

But it could take minutes to act. Minutes Milly didn't have.

Maskwa stepped closer and huffed again, her eyes like dark glass marbles. A paw flexed. Claws rasped against the cement floor.

Luther pointed his gun at the bear.

"*No!*" Milly stepped between him and Maskwa, arms wide. "Please. She doesn't deserve—" The bear's hot breath caressed her neck.

Fear numbed Milly. Her nose and eyes stung. She closed them. In a choked, thready voice, she began to sing a Russian lullaby. One her mother had sung to her. One she'd sung to Maskwa as a cub cuddled in her arms. A quiet acceptance fell over her.

The cage bars shuddered, accompanied by a screech of grinding metal. Milly's eyes blinked open.

"The panel, Milly!"

Luther and John, arms shaking with brute strength, had pulled the old lever down, lifting the panel to the sleeping area. Milly dove to the ground and scrambled through, bear behind her. Something sharp scraped her thigh.

With another loud groan, the heavy panel dropped like a guillotine. The bear cried out. Milly flipped over. The panel had caught Maskwa's shoulders, knocking her to her stomach. Milly met Maskwa's eyes and saw fear, such fear. Her old friend was trapped, afraid, and in pain.

The light in the bear's eyes faded. Her huge body melted.

"Open the door!" she screamed. It inched up and clicked into place.

Milly sobbed and rushed back to Maskwa. She knelt in front of the bear she'd helped save at birth, helped raise. Helped design. With tentative hands, she reached out to stroke her head, to comfort an animal that shouldn't exist.

She sang her lullaby to Maskwa until Luther touched her shoulder.

Milly stood and fell into his arms, weeping in relief and sorrow.

CHAPTER THIRTEEN

FOUR DAYS LATER

MILLY SAT in the lobby of the admin building with its raw finishes of wood and stone, soaring ceilings, and myriad of skylights. Her knee jiggled nervously, hands clutching the coat draped over her lap. She checked the clock above the reception desk for what seemed like the hundredth time.

Judgment day. The Pleistocene BioPark board meeting to determine Maskwa's fate. She'd been called in, expecting to be fired on the spot. To her great shock, that hadn't happened. Instead, she'd been asked to testify on behalf of the bear.

That didn't mean she'd gotten off scot-free. She'd received a side of harsh reprimand for her actions and the threat of *reassignment*. Grim, disapproving faces had looked down from a wall of large thinscreens as board members from all over the world lectured her about her reckless disregard for rules and regulations.

"All of your past reviews going back years praise your intelligence, levelheadedness, your quiet efficiency. You have been tagged as an extremely valuable, detail-oriented, if bor— um, *unexciting* employee who works above and beyond your tasks, but does so by the book," a stern-faced, steely-eyed woman said.

Boring. Milly lifted her chin. She vowed to wipe that word out of her employee file, starting immediately. "Then the person who filled out those reports doesn't really know me."

She kept her head high and came right back at them, decrying their distance—both physically and mentally—from vulnerable creatures they only saw in terms of monetary gain. Stiff expressions became stiffer, nostrils flared in anger at her scathing assessment. In the darkened room, Hialeah Kingbird dropped her head in her hands. Milly didn't care. Maskwa was important, not them. Not her.

"Everything I did was to help Maskwa, to relieve her suffering, to prove she was cruelly used by Doyle Amon. He exploited her pain and thousands of years of evolution, forcing her into conditions that required her to defend herself. Carin Zuanick's death is on his hands, not Maskwa's. She was only the tool he elected to use, the trigger he chose to pull. She doesn't deserve to die. Please. Let her live." Silence hung heavy as her plea faded away.

A thickly accented voice from a black screen weighed in ... and praised her.

"This young woman has the heart for our ark of creations that I wish to see in everyone involved in our zoo," he said. "She cares more for the animals than her job and her life. What you did to save that bear and discover Dr. Zuanick's murderer was dangerous, outrageous ... and courageous. Just what I expect from you, Dr. Smith."

Just what I expect. A faint frown puckered Milly's brows. What did he mean by that?

He finished in Russian. "Но больше так не делай, дорогая."

But don't do it again, my dear.

Milly swore she heard a smile in his voice.

And with that, she'd been asked to leave. She'd walked past a table of silent BioPark administrators, Hialeah Kingbird busy scribing on her thinscreen, not even deigning to raise her head. As Milly had exited through the huge carved doors, she'd passed Luther going in, who, polished and debonaire in a blue-gray silk suit, had acknowledged her with a probing glance. It was the first time she'd seen him since Maskwa's second surgery. Even though she'd kept her face placid, her breath had fluttered and cheeks heated.

This crush was ridiculous. Dr. Luther Nikolai was her boss and out of her league. Chin high, she'd strode past him in her red blouse and black slacks with the annoying button, which she swore she'd pitch into the trash when she finally got home. But that would have to wait.

She still had questions, and she was pretty sure Luther was the only one who would answer them. He was who she waited for now.

Milly glanced at the clock again—a whole minute had passed—when an elevator dinged and opened, disgorging half a dozen meeting participants, the rumble and pitch of their voices filling the void of sound. She stood as Luther appeared with Kingbird, the two deep in conversation as they exited. The BioPark director grabbed Luther by the arm and stopped him. He bent his head to hear whatever message she relayed, but his gaze roamed the lobby until it found Milly. There it rested as the conversation finished.

With a final nod, he left Kingbird and strode to Milly.

"You weren't fired."

"Do you know why?"

He hesitated before he answered. "I don't."

Milly drew in a shaky breath. "Their decision?"

"Not here. Let's head into the park and talk." He held out her jacket, and she slipped her arms into the sleeves. His hands seemed to linger, warm on her shoulders, before he opened the glass door for her to precede him outside.

She stepped into the chill fall day, clouds gravid with rain peppering the blue sky above. Snow was already accumulating in the high mountains that ringed the San Luis Valley.

"I'd like to check progress on the woolly rhinoceros exhibit," Luther said. "Would you prefer to walk or—"

"Walk."

They passed through an employee gate into the de-extinct cat quarter and strolled through the crowds of visitors. Even though her stomach constricted with worry for Maskwa, Milly smiled at the excited laughter of children when a pair of saber-toothed kittens, *Smilodon fatalis*, tumbled over each other in their exhibit, pouncing and crouching, pupils dark and round. A barking roar of an ancient mane-less American lion, *Panthera leo atrox*, was answered by a *Panthera spelaea*, the European cave lion last seen in paintings in the Lascaux and Chauvet caves in France. Keepers ran one of their animal ambas-sadors, a *Miracinonyx trumani*—American cheetah—using a retractable line with a "rabbit" to the awe of the crowd.

Luther Nikolai still hadn't spoken as they headed into the heart of the BioPark, but, Milly noted, he'd relaxed. Her worry lifted a little. Still, he surprised her when he stopped at a vendor cart and bought her a mammoth-shaped balloon made up of aqueous-dissolvable film in case one dropped inside an exhibit and was eaten. He bought pink cotton candy for himself, with the deprecating comment, "Sweet tooth."

The wind tugged at her large balloon as they strolled up a gently inclined path, bumping it against one of a cute giant sloth tethered to a stroller. Head tipped back, the bundled-up, dark-haired toddler squirmed and stretched arms to reach it.

Luther finally spoke.

"Maskwa will not be euthanized."

Milly closed her eyes. A wave of relief weakened her knees.

"However, it was decided she cannot remain here. She'll be sent to Siberia and put in the care of rewilding specialists for eventual release into their Pleistocene BioPark wilderness region."

"But that's millions of acres of untamed land. She's never been exposed to the wild. She's never hunted, never had to defend herself or territory—"

"It was the best I could do," he said gently. "John Radebe and Sabrina Navas will be traveling with Maskwa. They have agreed to transfer to Siberia after we threatened Navas with attempted murder. Thank goodness you turned that camera on. I think John was relieved they would be given a fresh start. He's invested in becoming a father."

Milly suppressed the protests that trembled on her lips. Maskwa would live. John would watch over her. And Sabrina ... "How is Sabrina?"

"Extremely remorseful, at least that's what our psychologists tell us. They have also diagnosed Navas as bipolar with narcissistic personality disorder. She's back on her meds, although I would ask you to keep this information to yourself. I thought you deserved to know since she did try to kill you." He paused. "Are you all right with these decisions?"

"Yes. And I'm glad. Everyone should get a second chance."

"You're more forgiving than I." He gazed toward a huge mesh enclosure surrounding a copse of tall trees. Inside, a golden-hued *Gigantopithecus blacki* sat like a Buddha on a high platform, face raised to the sun. "In Siberia, Radebe will be trained in rewilding, and Navas will be given a position teaching at the veterinarian college if she can pass a written exam—in Spanish this time." He smiled. "We'll see if her big talk equals actual knowledge."

They meandered through paved trails for a few minutes before Milly asked, "When do they leave?"

"When Maskwa has completely healed. A month, maybe. You know she's recovering?"

Milly nodded. She'd been pivotal in getting the bear back into an aboveground off-exhibit enclosure so she could bask in the sunshine and grub in the dirt.

"What about the police investigation of Carin's death?" she asked. "They wanted the bullet you said was buried in Maskwa's, er, fat pad. The nonexistent one." She raised her brows.

He laughed but sobered quickly. "If the board voted for euthanasia, I had a bullet ready. Before I staged the shooting in the surgical suite, I went to the meat storage warehouse and shot a side of beef, then dipped it in Maskwa's blood. Now the police will never get that bullet, and, hopefully, their investigation will be closed."

Milly wasn't so sure that Natalia Roman would let it go so easily. The detective had been deeply suspicious during that initial interview. Milly doubted this would be the last they'd see of her and her silent companion.

She and Luther separated to allow a line of red-T-shirted children snake between them, two by two. Each held aloft balloons of various de-extincts.

When the children had passed, Milly asked, "Why did Carin invite you to the surgery?" Though she suspected she knew why, she wanted to hear the answer directly from him.

"I couldn't tell you earlier because it was a personnel issue, but now ... She wanted me to observe both Gavin Appleton and Sabrina Navas. She'd heard persistent rumors about Appleton's forgetfulness and that the residents and techs were covering for him. And Carin had noted problems with Navas's mental health. She wanted me to see firsthand." His voice hardened. "That she was potentially putting others in danger was reckless and stupid and pure Carin. I should have stopped the surgery as soon as I arrived, especially when—"

Milly waited, but he didn't complete his thought. She finished for him.

"When you found me there instead of Appleton. Why did you care?" She held her breath for his answer, kicking herself.

He took a moment to reply. "For no other reason than I'm your supervisor. Your well-being is important to my genetics program." His gaze rested on her upturned face. "Do you understand, Dr. Smith?"

The Christmas party all over again. *That kiss was a mistake. Too much celebratory vodka. My apologies.* Her foolish ache of longing faded.

"Perfectly, Dr. Nikolai," she said, proud of the steady calm in her voice. Thank goodness she'd already decided to keep him at arm's length. She wound the ribbon holding the balloon around her wrist. "Dr. Kingbird drugged me after that first surgery. She induced my retrograde amnesia."

"*That* I did not agree to. How did you find out?"

Anger tightened her jaw. "You just told me. And something Appleton said. Why did she do it?"

"Because the board is very outside-authority adverse, and Kingbird knew you wouldn't let this rest because the de-extincts are so important to you. Yet you still dug."

"The outside authorities—Detective Roman and her partner—don't even know about Amon's involvement, do they?"

"The board has decided that everything that's occurred since Carin's death would be better handled in-house."

As if the BioPark were its own sovereign country. No wonder at Detective Roman's frustration.

"Carin was your wife once. It wasn't important to you to know the truth?"

"Yes, but I was warned off early and very explicitly—my job threatened because of my actions during the revival protocol."

"You tried to let Carin and me out," she said. Amon *had* lied to her.

"The board was quite furious about that because if Maskwa had escaped, they could have been exposed to, uh, greater liability." He chuckled mirthlessly. "Their threat made my investigation more difficult. Even so, between the two of us ... maybe next time we should work together."

His half smile was back but clearly indulgent. He didn't think there'd be a next time. They'd make a good team, though—her with her attention to detail, him with a big-picture view. Still, it would be better if she maintained a professional distance.

"But this is all hindsight analysis. You obviously found evidence we missed." He stopped to drop his half-eaten cotton candy into a trash receptacle and turned to her, his gaze lingering. "We continue to underestimate you, Dr. Ludmilla Smith."

"Because I'm so boring?"

He chuckled. "Not boring."

Her skin zinged and warmed.

He was mentally stroking her, she knew. Drawing her away from her anger at the way she'd been manipulated. She did feel a sense of pride that she'd out-thought him, though, had seen things that he'd missed.

That Luther Nikolai was human.

They began walking again.

"You already knew about the second surgery before I texted, didn't you?" she said. "After I left John's house, he called you."

He nodded. "To tell me you'd figured out much of what had happened, including the e-gun switch and that *someone* had exchanged the flash-stick drugs." He slid her a glance. "Something I did not know. He then informed me that he was helping you because he owed it to Carin and the bear, and that if I had an ounce of compassion left and hadn't completely sold my soul to the BioPark administration, I'd stay out of it. The second time that day someone tore me a—uh, *excoriated* me over what I'd become. After some internal reflection, I'm ashamed to say you are both correct."

"You cleaned up Maskwa for her surgery and made sure the room was warm."

"And waited on edge for John's call that the surgery was over and a success. What I didn't expect was a text from you telling me that you had a plan to relieve Maskwa's pain *and* catch the murderer. That was stupid of you, Milly."

Her cheeks heated at the withering edge in his voice. She lifted her chin and brazened it out.

"Sometimes people do stupid things to help those they love. Besides, it worked, didn't it? Well, almost."

Luther's eyes narrowed. His lips thinned. She rushed on before he could excoriate *her*.

"For only being at the BioPark a few weeks, Amon did his homework. He knew about the extra syringe of sedative I always keep in my pocket, which, I assume, he picked when he bumped into me racing out of the suite. Something I might have figured out earlier if I hadn't been drugged," she finished sourly.

He nodded, expression softening.

"And I'm certain the antibiotic I administered to Maskwa during the first surgery was mixed with antidote. The contents of that syringe were never tested?"

"It was destroyed. When Detective Roman asked, we blamed the loss of evidence on the chaos and the necessity of extracting the bear, you, and Carin's body. But we did test the contents of the syringe you confiscated from Amon during the second surgery. It contained antidote." He clasped his hands behind his back. "Or perhaps he could have used the e-gun you so conveniently brought? Attempting to catch him with his own trick?"

"Well, yes, especially after I confronted him. But Sabrina Navas stepped right in the middle, a detail I didn't plan for." She sighed. "Amon's still missing?"

After Milly's rescue, John had found Sabrina alone and unharmed down a dark passage. Security had attempted to follow Doyle Amon's trail, but with no luck.

"We believe he's left the BioPark," Luther said.

"But you're not sure." Homeless people and thrill-seekers had been found living deep in some of the defunct underground corridors and rooms, a labyrinth rivaling that of the mythical Minotaur.

"If he's still around and you truly are his target, he's dangerous. You need to be careful," Luther warned.

"Who is Doyle Amon?"

"An alias with meticulous paperwork. I'm still researching his background, with very little luck. He's covered his tracks well. But his name should have been a clue. Doyle is derived from an Irish surname meaning 'dark stranger,' and Amon is Greek for 'hidden one.'"

"I think he was in the Russian military, too."

Luther's eyes shuttered. "Why didn't you say anything about that to the board?"

"Because I have no evidence to back it up. I don't even know him." She paused, then pressed him. "Was I Doyle Amon's true target? Why would anyone want me dead?"

"Milly, I—" His wrist tech buzzed. Frowning, he touched the screen. His face lost color. "Amon's tracking app just activated. He's in the park. He's following us." He glanced behind them, then grabbed Milly's arm, hustling her up the path.

"Why would he activate his tech now when everyone's looking for him? Besides, he told me he only wore it around Dr. Appleton—"

The punch of two shots tore through the air. Luther shoved Milly down and covered her with his body. Balloons and birds lifted into the sky, accompanied by the squawks of animals and screams of BioPark guests. She'd reflexly released her balloon, too. It floated up, pulled out of sight by the breeze. Milly refocused her gaze on the man pressing her into the hard ground.

Luther stared down at her, sharing her breath, his heart beating in time with hers.

"You're all right?"

She nodded, mouth dry. "Just caught between the Scylla and Charybdis," she murmured. "I had to look that up, you know."

His body relaxed, relief and something she couldn't define passing over his face. He levered up and pulled her to her feet.

Another buzz of his wrist tech. Tapping it, Luther frowned as he stared at the screen. "This doesn't make sense." He drew a gun from inside his jacket.

Milly's eyes widened. "What's going on?"

"Stay here," he ordered and ran toward where the shots had sounded.

She hesitated for only a moment before charging after him.

Dodging hunkered and panicked guests, she barely kept him in sight. He topped the hill and dropped into the vendor grotto. She followed, out of breath when she finally caught up to him.

Luther threw a scowl in her direction, then focused on the dead man sprawled next to a balloon-and-popcorn vendor's cart. His chest contained a bloody hole, and the back of his head was gone from the bullet between his sightless brown eyes with their ring of gray blue.

"I guess I won't have to worry about Doyle Amon anymore," Milly said. "But who shot him?"

EPILOGUE

BEHIND A SCREEN OF LEAVES, SHE SHIVERS. THE HARD bang of sound still rings in her ears, mixing with screams and cries and the screech and flutter of lifting birds. Air-balls swirl up, their shadows crossing over her watchful face, thin tails tangling into the tree branches above.

She saw one of theirs as he ran away until she could see him no more. She sees the same one of theirs lying down. He doesn't move.

A swirl of wind brings her smoke and blood. She inhales deeply and stirs. Hands tuck closely to her chest. She moves her fingers as she's been taught, forming what none of hers can understand, only theirs.

i see

i saw

EXCERPT: SIGNS
A DE-EXTINCT ZOO MYSTERY

CHAPTER ONE

Pleistocene BioPark
  San Luis Valley, New Mexico and Colorado, USA
  Mammoth Auditorium
  Wednesday, 7:26 P.M.

Milly's only warning before Luther Nikolai's warm breath touched her ear was the demand of his hand circling her wrist. Electricity crackled over her skin.

"Do you see him? Coming straight up the middle, like a profane Moses parting the Red Sea." Luther kept his voice low in deference to the ongoing slide presentation by Hialeah Kingbird, the Pleistocene BioPark's director. He sat in the folding chair next to Milly's on the shadowy stage, nearest the lectern. "Minchin Spears. A snake cloaked in the piety of the press. He's nothing but toxic."

Milly Smith, senior veterinary resident at the BioPark, forced away Luther's effect on her ability to think and peered through light reflected from the slides into the auditorium. She'd normally be in a row farther back, but her supervisor was on an extended vacation and she'd been directed to substitute for him during the Q and A portion of the program.

From her front-row seat, it was easy to spot Spears's signature fluorescent green-blond hair. He waltzed through the tightly packed audience of fellow journalists and reporters who deferentially stepped aside, a few even extending hands to touch his darkly iridescent suit, perhaps hoping some of his celebrity would rub off on them. Thinscreens lifted above heads to record his progress, and excited murmurs whirred through the crowd, masking Kingbird's barely discernible midsentence pause before she continued her presentation on the ongoing construction of the woolly rhino exhibit. She wouldn't be happy Minchin Spears was making her scheduled outreach to the media all about Minchin Spears.

Luther's sigh hissed. "After out last confron—*encounter*, I personally requested that жóпa be banned from future releases."

"No. You requested he be thrown to the *Smilodon*s." Milly raised an eyebrow, lips curving into a smile. "Or was it impaled on a woolly rhino horn?"

She turned her head just enough to trace Luther's shaved scalp and bold profile. He looked good tonight, as usual. Gray-blue dress shirt hugging his muscled shoulders and chest, trousers with knifepoint creases under sinewed hands balled into fists on his thighs. She, on the other hand …

Her fingers picked at a pill of material on her barely acceptable black slacks. She resisted the urge to pull it off, which would probably cause an embarrassing unravel. Her red blouse was in a little better shape, except for the frayed cuffs she'd hidden by rolling up her sleeves. She really needed to buy new clothes. Scrubs, sweats, and T-shirts didn't properly represent senior members of the BioPark staff, or so said an email warning sent from Kingbird's office.

"Eaten by *Smilodon*s, gored by rhinos, *and* suspended by his ankles over the *Quinkana* lagoon," said a low voice from behind Milly. A sugary bubble gum scent preceded the scrape of a chair as Felicity Top, head *Gigantopithecus blacki* keeper, scooted closer. "You said you wanted to see high how those crocs could jump if properly motivated."

Felicity's gum popped between her teeth. "And he might be toxic, but he's *way* too valuable to the BioPark to ever be banned. He was one of the first holocast influencers, you know. A billion followers clambering to see whichever controversial de-extinct he spotlights. He's affiliate, too. Makes coin off ticket sales, plus other perks. You know the board gives him an annual pass? He practically lives here. And I heard he's behind the donations for the playground equipment after that ass Horace wrecked the last set. He's been hanging around the giganto enclosure enough lately." Felicity touched Milly's shoulder. "You're coming by tomorrow morning to do Elizabeth Barrett's ultrasound, right?"

"Early, if possible," Milly answered as Kingbird finished at exactly seven-thirty with an appeal for any questions. Applause pattered from the audience, and the lights brightened, dimming the AI hologram used to translate Kingbird's talk to ASL. Milly straightened, ready in case she was called to answer inquiries about the de-extincts in her care, including how Maskwa, the short-faced bear, was doing at her new home in Siberia. Thriving, thank goodness, under keeper John Radebe's supervision.

A reporter Milly recognized from a Denver entertainment feed was handed the microphone.

"My question is for the head of your de-extinction genetics program. Dr. Nikolai?"

Luther stood and strode to the front of the stage. The woman smiled, her eyes devouring him with all the verve of a *Mustela nivalis*— Least Weasel—tracking prey. She even looked like one with her russet hair and slinky physique.

Milly unclenched her fingers, hating the bead of jealousy that formed in her chest. A stupid and futile emotion. Luther evinced nothing but a professional interest in her, except for a single alcohol-fueled kiss almost a year ago. A mistake, he'd murmured, and backed away with unflattering speed to mix with guests at his annual Christmas party as if he hadn't just shattered her evening and her heart. Their interactions since she'd solved the murder of his ex-wife and saved Maskwa's life a month earlier had been cordial, even if she found him studying her sometimes.

Minchin Spears stepped up beside the weas—*woman*—and plucked the microphone from her hands. Her puffy lips and heavily lashed eyes formed three perfect O's of surprise. He tugged an orange-spotted pink handkerchief from the pocket of his iridescent blue-green blazer and waved it like a flag in her face.

"Wipe the drool off your chin, darling. The eminent Doctor Luther Anton Maksim Nikolai isn't interested in you." He spoke into the microphone, capitalizing on his rapt audience, every word out of his mouth a performance. Tut-tutting, he examined her smooth forehead, straight nose, and lifted breasts. "He deals with better modifications every day. Genetic, of course, and not elective as are yours. Thus, he prefers something more ... natural."

Titters and gasps of outrage filled the room. Milly shifted to Luther's empty chair for a better view when Spears's green eyes, sharp as broken glass, pinned her in place. He winked. Minchin Spears, she decided, would be right at home with the *Quinkanas*.

"Mr. Spears." Luther clasped his hands behind his back. "I wish I could say it was nice to see you again."

Sound swelled across the audience followed by an immediate shushing until Milly could hear the rustle of clothing as the crowd bent nearer. Hialeah Kingbird stood behind Luther, her face expressionless but tight. How long would it be before she'd need to intervene this time?

"And me so charming! But I digress, so I'll get straight to the point." Spears shifted the microphone in his hand, his whole aspect hardening. "A month ago, a lowly vet tech was murdered at your lovely zoo. I'm sure you remember, as you and the delightful Dr. Smith arrived first on scene. And while the official investigation has stalled, I've uncovered some very interesting information about the dead man and, perhaps, why he was targeted for assassination."

"Then, perhaps, you should tell your story to the police," Luther said.

Minchin Spears smiled. It wasn't pleasant. "As you know, there were no, ah, witnesses. All those people around: children, families, staff. CCTV. And no one saw a thing."

Kingbird stepped out from her lectern. Behind her on the screen, the AI interpreter's hands stayed quiet. Kingbird must have turned it off. "Mr. Spears, we've been thoroughly updated on the investigation into Doyle Amon's death."

Minchin Spears continued as if Kingbird hadn't spoken. "Or did *someone* see *everything*?" As if by magic, a deep purple book appeared in his hand. An actual book, not a thinscreen. He riffled the paper, opening to a page.

Crowd noise rose, starting in the back of the auditorium. The murmurings rippled forward like a cresting wave as spectators divided. The head of BioPark security, Jim Daisy, and two of his men bulled their way to the front.

Spears pivoted his torso to assess the renewed muttering behind him. The book in his hand disappeared. He switched off the microphone and bellied up to the stage, gesturing for Nikolai to come closer. Luther dropped to one knee. Milly, perched on the edge of her seat, strained to hear, but noise in the room swelled again. She focused on Spears's lips.

... know what ... 're hiding. Meet me at—

Luther shifted, blocking Milly's view.

"Look at Kingbird," Felicity whispered. Milly turned. She wasn't the only one trying to read Minchin Spears's lips.

Luther pushed to his feet, eyes glittering, face unyielding. He spun and strode off the stage without a backward glance. The crowd surged forward, screaming questions at Luther's retreat, demanding to know what he, Spears, or anyone else knew about the murder. Although her gaze followed Luther, Hialeah Kingbird stood firm. The director knew better than to rush after him and add fuel to an already explosive environment.

Security reached Minchin Spears. Jim Daisy grasped the man's elbow and leaned in to speak. Two other officers flanked them. Spears pulled away from Daisy and all four pushed through the audience to a side exit, Daisy closing the door behind them.

A screeching, nails-on-chalkboard feedback from the microphone whipped the attention of the churning crowd back to Kingbird. She raised her hands and smiled indulgently. "Mr. Spears always entertains, does he not? I know you have a lot of questions, but I'd like you to hold them until after I present the three-dimensional model of our soon-to-be-completed woolly rhino exhibit."

Once the lights came down again, so did the volume. A neat trick Kingbird had employed more than once. Like blindfolding an animal.

Milly swiveled in her seat, eyes probing the shadows behind her for Luther. She wasn't the only one. Half the assembled staff peered into the shrouded stage. The other half whispered and gossiped. Except Felicity. She relaxed in her chair, arms crossed over her heavy bosom, popping her gum.

Milly swung around and sat forward, knees and heels together, hands clasped in her lap. Luther was gone, disappearing with much less fanfare than Minchin Spears and his purple book.

What worried her was the split-second glimpse she'd had of Luther. He'd looked ready to commit murder.

ALSO BY CAROL POTENZA

Nicky Matthews Mysteries

Hearts of the Missing

The Third Warrior

Spirit Daughters

Coming 2024: Sacred Ghosts

De-Extinct Zoo Mystery Series

Unmasked

Signs

Coming 2024: Ambushed

Lies Mystery Series

Coming Fall 2023: Sting of Lies

Non-Fiction

Demystifying the Beats: How to Write a Killer Book

IF YOU ENJOYED THIS BOOK...

Authors live for honest reviews. They help other readers find their work in a world where millions of books are published each year. If you enjoyed this story or any other of my books and have a few minutes, please leave a quick review at Amazon, Barnes and Noble, Kobo, Google, or even on my website...

Short or long, your words can make all the difference.

Thank you.

ACKNOWLEDGMENTS

Writing a book is a team effort and I'm so glad I don't have to do it alone. I want to thank my critique partners, my editor, my proofreader, my cover artist, and my beta readers, SS and AP. I can't tell you how much you all made this story better.

ABOUT THE AUTHOR

Carol Potenza is a scientist, a reader, and a mystery author. Her wide-ranging scientific research for her classes and her stories led her to the absolute truth that she would do (almost) anything to visit a zoo that has a live de-extinct mammoth, while the reader inside her made her believe she could write murder mysteries. She lives in the beautiful state of New Mexico with her patient husband, Leos, and her chihuahua, Hermes, who snoozes in a doggie beanbag next to her as she writes until he's ready for a walk. Then he won't leave her alone.

For more books and updates visit:
carolpotenza.com

Made in the USA
Middletown, DE
09 November 2024

64204419R00062